Amber was born in February 2000 and lives in the south coast of England. *The Above* is her first book, the idea of which first emerged when she was 15. She is currently studying at university.

This book is dedicated to Britney Timera Henry, my best friend for ever (and yes, now everyone knows your middle name).

Amber-Rose Knowlton

The Above

AUSTIN MACAULEY PUBLISHERS™

LONDON ∗ CAMBRIDGE ∗ NEW YORK ∗ SHARJAH

A CIP catalogue record for this title is available from the British Library.

ISBN 9781528986748 (Paperback)
ISBN 9781528986755 (ePub e-book)

www.austinmacauley.com

First Published (2021)
Austin Macauley Publishers Ltd
25 Canada Square
Canary Wharf
London
E14 5LQ

There are a few amazing people who helped encourage and support me through not only the writing of this book, but through life in general. If it were not for them, and if it were not for God, I do not believe I would have the courage to do what I do. First and foremost, I would like to thank Britney for being an absolute star and supporting me in times of stress and sadness. You have been my rock when I didn't think the storms in my life were going to end, you have made me laugh when no one else could, and you have always been brutally honest with me. Thank you for reading parts of my book and promising to be honest in the way of criticism and for helping me to develop my ideas with your unbelievably smart mind. Furthermore, thank you, Mum, Paps, and Kate. As parents, you have been so supportive of everything I do in life, especially in writing this book. Mum, you have supported me financially and emotionally, and you are one of the strongest women I know. Paps, your terrible dad jokes and constant excitement about the publishing of this book have never failed to make me laugh. The same goes for the rest of my family; thank you all for being the weird but amazing people that you are. And Jasmine, my little but wise sister, without you I would 'never' be where I am now. Sapphire, without your weirdness and creativity, I would not laugh as much as I do each day. Thank you also to my housemates at university: Rebekah Aust, Naomi Spiers, Tamara Lane, and Charis Mccobb. You all may not have known it, but you yourselves helped me continue to write this book simply because of your consistent positivity and faith. You pray over me whenever I go through trials in life, and I need those prayers more than you know. I finally want to thank the people I have met in my life during the very final editing stages of this book. Thank you to everyone at UoW busking society. Joining you guys has been a roller coaster, but it has helped me reveal my creative side even more, and gain more courage. Thank you to Charlie Wilson, who I met during the very final editing stages of this book. I can honestly say that I have never met a man more caring, selfless, and loving. You make me laugh and smile unfailingly, and you are there when I need you. I adore doing life with you, and want to do life with you for as long as I am able. And last but not at all least, thank you to my course mates, Paulina Dumciute, Sabrina

Daniels, Joe Boulay, Dani Smith, Shan Fisher, and Max German, who are not just my course mates, but my best friends too. They bring so much laughter to me every day. Thank you to everyone at the publishing team who made this possible. Oh, also, let's not forget God, because ya know, I would not be here without you (literally) and you will never leave me in this crazy thing which is life. I hope you all enjoy reading this book as much as I enjoy doing life with you.

Prologue

"Oh God," a father repeated over and over, his response perhaps too insignificant for the sudden abrupt change in weather conditions. Amid summer, it is completely unseasonable for snow to pulsate down on the heads of the surrounding population. "Oh God, *no*."

The father's young boy stood with his parents and younger sister in London, which ten minutes earlier had been around twenty-nine degrees.

"Liam, Son, do not let go of your mother's hands." Liam struggled to adjust as the cold slithered across his every bone.

They had been queuing to ride the London eye, although it was only a queue as little as five others. The city seemed near apocalyptic; everyone had been in their houses for weeks after all. But, looking at the river and sky and buildings, the small children still thought there was beauty in it, their eyes filled with only awe and curiosity towards the world around them.

Liam clutched his mother's hand a bit tighter, looking up at his sister of just three years. Riley was only moments ago laughing at their father pulling silly faces, but then even she was confused when everything turned abruptly from sun-filled skies to a blanket of white.

It was August.

The mother, who was beautiful with slight colour in her cheeks and brown hair which fell gracefully behind her shoulders, held worry in her own eyes that was not there before. But unlike her children, she seemed to understand what was happening more than she perhaps should have done. An understanding that led her to carry frustration at something or someone.

Liam looked at her, then at his father, and then back at her again. His father, too, held worry in his own eyes. The boy, smarter than the average boy his age, saw something else in his father's eyes too.

Guilt?

The small number of people around them grew confused, and then held fear as the slight bitter cold rapidly became closer to a storm, an unbearable wind surfacing in the London air.

Liam watched those around him intently, and their cries and tears and screams which had started to emerge almost instantaneously stopped, as if they had never occurred in the first place. Their faces became emotionless. They walked, with a seemingly newfound determination, through the storm and in the same direction as one another.

As though they were following a silent order.

Liam's family did not move like other people. Neither did one child that Liam spotted in the distance, around the same age as him but with messy hair and big, innocent green eyes. This child called out to his parents, but they did not even turn back to look in his direction.

Liam was about to reach out towards the other child, deeply sensing something that was entirely wrong, but his mouth was suddenly covered by his father's hand. The boy looked up to see his sister's mouth and nose also covered desperately. His mother was urged to do the same herself, and she did so. They seemed to be making barriers between their lungs and the cold air, as though they were infected by something.

For a long second, the father paused and took a deep breath, while waiting cautiously as though he held a small expectancy for something to happen to himself. When he appeared satisfied that what he thought could happen did not, he picked up the young girl from the mother's arm and pulled them both urgently.

"Come on, Emelia, we need to leave. *Now.* It's only a matter of time." A newfound urgency was present in his face; the concern ran deep. Through the storm they ran, but Emelia's reluctance was strong.

"You knew! You knew this was going to happen to all these people." She gestured back towards those whom they had been so close to just moments ago, her hands shaking from cold or fear.

"*You* knew and you didn't try to stop it, James!" The weather was too strong for James to see the tears welling up in her brown eyes, which soon turned to small icicles. With a change of tone, between sobs she cried; "We're leaving so many people behind."

"I didn't know it would be like *this*! I never wanted it to be like this," he hoarsely screamed in reply while he scanned the small number of people who had somehow transformed into crowds, walking determinedly through the harsh wind like soldiers.

"Maybe it'll be for the better," his voice, being now a whisper, was barely conceivable in the breeze. He didn't seem so sure.

Only James seemed to know exactly what was happening to these people. In his head, he heard the voice of the man who had once been his friend. *It's for the good of the people, James. They are protected like this.* He had once believed these words, but at that moment, holding his family in his arms and squinting through the wind, the words seemed far from true. The wind picked up, but Liam did not notice. He turned and behind him was the other boy still calling out desperately for his family which were clearly gone.

Liam shouted towards him. He failed to hear anything even though he was mouthing the words clearly, but his voice may have just been lost by the sound of the storm. He shouted again, with such force that his entire body shook, causing him to lose the grip of his mother's hand. She was oblivious to this; her hands were so numb from the cold that the only thing she could feel was her heart beating rapidly against her chest. Riley, who was the only one that noticed, locked wide eyes with her brother and began to cry hopelessly with love and desperation.

Liam fell to his knees.

In James' peripheral vision, he saw the barely visible manhole cover on the ground, lifted it, and urged his confused family inside.

Still, he did not notice his son was gone, his eyes clouded with white. He did not see his own son with his head in his knees, hugging them tightly against the full force of snow.

Liam began losing the colour from his cheeks.

"What have they done? What have I done!" his father screamed as he entered the sewer, which revealed not a sewer but instead, an underground series of small, office-like rooms.

The government's actions had to be kept undisclosed, so all those involved were permitted to finding somewhere they could carry out their part with no risk of exposure. James had built an office underground which he had once been proud of, but now he trembled as he paced it numbly.

Behind him, Liam felt hands shaking his shoulder.

"Come on!" the child he had seen earlier was now behind him, piercing green eyes keeping a hold of his own, small lungs screaming desperately through the wind.

"I'm Noah, but now isn't the time for introductions. We gotta go, okay?"

The family stopped, panted, took their hands away from their mouths as they reached the ground.

Riley continued to cry.

The two boys ran, unknowingly, towards the direction the other people had walked. They noticed more people walking that way too, seemingly emotionless. Their calls meant nothing to the people as they followed, and they were oblivious to the world they were about to encounter.

"Where's Liam?" Emelia asked so quickly that her words combined into one.

The children heard voices as they ran. They wanted to feel hope, but the voices were not comforting. They were robot-like, emotionless, monotone.

Riley's eyes widened, and her sobs echoed around the underground room with tears of unimaginable sadness, her small arms reaching to the world above.

The storm died down enough so that, in front of them, the boys saw a line of hundreds or thousands of other children and adults and middle-aged men and women, stood tall. Liam took a step forward as the line of people shortened, until soon he was right in front. In fear, he mimicked the emotionless people around him. He held out his arm obediently, tried not to wince at the pain of the needle. Instead, he just looked straight ahead and accepted the sharp pain that pierced his delicate skin.

Tattooed permanently on the boy's small, delicate wrist, the words read: *SOLDIER 111*

"He's gone."

Chapter One

15 Years Later

I don't remember a significant amount about the Above, but there's a lot I guess I know.

I know that there are five oceans on Earth, and in these oceans, there are between seven hundred thousand and one million species. I know that I live underground in the country of England, which is covered by around three million hectares of woodland, home to insects and foxes and wide-eyed deer. I know that at night, if you take away all the pollution and look past the tall buildings, you can see thousands of stars (and sometimes some planets) in the sky. I know that fifteen years ago, there was a population of around sixty million people in the United Kingdom, all with their own unique passions and beliefs and opportunities and families and fates.

Population now?

Uncertain.

Little did I know it then, but I used to be a part of that extraordinary phenomenon of a world. My father says it isn't like that anymore though. He says it has changed since the storm.

I still wish, just sometimes, I could escape from these underground walls just to breathe the air from the Above. The air that is new and old to me, both at the same time. But I stay here for my family.

I stay here because I don't want my parents to lose another child.

I vaguely remember a time when I was much younger; my mother sat with me by the fire in our living room, while we relished the intensity of the warmth. I looked out the window at the sky, the beauty of it, and admired how everything outside was so different. There didn't appear to be a single way that everyone and everything was living. Everything was so diverse. I think my mother held the same wonder and awe that I held that day, if not every day.

My father, however, sat at the table, eyebrows furrowed, and looked sternly at that day's newspaper. I think maybe there were little beads of sweat rolling down his forehead, but I do not think it was from the heat of the fire, rather it was from stress. Liam, my older brother, asked him questions like: 'Should we not go outside anymore?' or 'Are we safe?' and my father replied, "I will do whatever is necessary to protect us all."

I do not remember much of how my life had been before the storm, the night when everything turned cold and dark. But even though, at around three years of age, I didn't understand a lot, I remember the news, consistent terror and worry, and my father's undivided focus on something that I was clearly oblivious to. This obliviousness could have been the result of one of two things: my age, or that I was never meant to find out what was going on.

My mother sometimes used to sneak me and Liam outside of the house when it was dusk, and my father was asleep. Those were the days which neared closer to the storm, the days when the number of people outside declined at an unbelievable rate, and I am not sure why, other than the fear that captured them all for some unknown reason.

I cannot remember holding fear on days like those. I would spin around and stare up at the sky until I was dizzy, arms outstretched, and I would laugh and say things that I guess three-year olds would say, silly things that made my mother laugh.

The day my brother fell and didn't get back up, the day of the storm, is the only other day I seem to remember from before.

I screamed and he screamed, and we were not heard amid the raging wind. I was carried while my parents ran to my new home, here underneath.

There was a chair and a desk, blankets, and notes when we got here. My father said he would come here before the storm and work privately when he had to work on some kind of top-secret business. I had learnt not to question him about his job before everything happened, but instead focus on his job now, which I guess is simply survival. I help with that job too, in a small kind of way, walking around these four walls day and night helping to make our home safe and comfortable. It gets a little tedious; I'd rather go to the Above and help my father collect food and water, but he won't let me.

I have been here long enough that I do not even have to open my eyes to navigate myself around. I have been here long enough to know everything that is here.

Everything.

Though I guess it's really not that impressive, because these walls don't expand much further than a few hundred metres.

I wake in a start, already wrapped in an oversized jumper, and yet still reach for the additional warmth of my blanket which is loosely covering my body.

Around me, it is clear to see not much has changed since we came here fifteen years ago. Other than the decrease in the amount of food we have, which fluctuates weekly, it is almost identical. Yet, every time I open my eyes, I hold my breath before opening them just in case something *has* changed.

It never does.

My own small room holds only a few blankets, clothes and a flask for water. It is dark as it is every morning, but a small amount of grey light escapes from cracks in the ceiling. Some also tiptoes around the corner and embraces me, telling me that the morning fire is lit.

The warm smell of sugar fills the air which is a rarity as our breakfast mostly consists of any remnants of food that we have left or that my father can find when he is in the Above. Stale bread is usually probable, but I guess it's okay if you imagine the bread is something else when you are eating it.

I get up and walk through to the next room, which is only marginally bigger than my own.

My mother, with tired lines under her eyes and a warm smile, looks up from above the fire. The hushed conversation in which she was having with my father beside her is quickly finished, as always. And as always, I pretend to be oblivious to it.

They are huddled up closely, partially because it is cold, but mostly because they seek each other's company.

"Hey, Ri," my father says, with clear exhaustion in his voice. But there is a small underlying happiness too, as if just me being there brings him alleviation.

I walk over to the corner and grab some chalk, then lean my head against the wall and reach to make a mark. When I move away, I am still only five foot and two inches. My mother chuckles and says, "Riley, you're eighteen, sweetheart. You aren't going to grow any taller." But I think maybe it's just because we are malnourished, which has hindered my desired growth spurt. I stand on my tiptoes and draw a line that is about an inch above my actual height, marking it as *5'3"*. This makes my mother laugh even more.

Then I draw us as stick people under the stars, and Liam is there too.

Sometimes, I tell our stories on these walls. Not that there's much to tell, but I often make stories up of what could have been, what would have been if nothing had changed since I was young. I've drawn my first non-existent relationship and, consequently, my first non-existent heartbreak, followed by heaps of ice cream which I no longer remember the taste of. I've drawn my brother's non-existent university graduation, followed by my own non-existent university graduation. I've drawn our non-existent first jobs, and our non-existent marriages, and family dinners and events.

All completely and unfortunately not real.

My father continues to speak as I perch myself behind both my parents and sigh, my dreams of a normal reality coming to a quick close.

"I've made you breakfast. As soon as you've finished, I'd like you to help your mother boil the water. You'll need to wash your clothes." In response to his remark, my eyes gaze down to my clothes which are clearly in need of a wash. It is hard to do this often when you only own two pairs of trousers and two knit jumpers, one of which barely fits you.

. I sit beside our fire, adjusting my position for a long time to make sure that I don't sit on my endlessly long brown hair. Eventually I give up and sigh, sitting cross-legged with my hair in about every inch of open floor space around us, some tucked behind my ears. My mother sighs, but it is the sort of light-hearted sigh you receive when the sigher finds you somewhat amusing. She hands me an old scrunchie from her wrist, so I smile and tie my hair up accordingly.

After breakfast, I boil the water which my father collects from the snow in the Above. He uses old buckets to collect it when he leaves, and it stays in the solid form of snow right up until it is boiled.

Then I undress, skin cold shades of white and blue, and pour cups of hot water over my arms and legs. My collarbones are prominent from lack of food, and I can trace the outline of my ribcage. Following that, I wash my clothes and sit wrapped in an old towel, letting them dry by the fire while I hug my knees tightly to my chest.

My father grabs a hold of his desk chair and drags it along the floor so that it is inline directly with the manhole cover above us. He climbs out after promising he won't be long and that he loves us, then leaves.

It's often not long before he returns with more firewood and food. Sometimes, he takes longer; a week, two. Never quite more than three.

16

For each day he is gone, I finish around two books. I own only a shelf full, but I am always relentlessly thankful they are there. They may only seem like several hundred white pages, all gentle to my fingertips. But they are my wisdom and my escape from all I've ever known, each compelling sentence feeding the liveliness of my brain.

The Above sounds beautiful in each book I read. It sounds like somewhere I would want to live, not hide from. I can almost feel the sun on my face, the wind lifting me from my feet. I can almost remember the nights that my three-year old self-span around, feeling the night's air and hearing my mother and Liam's laughter.

When my father takes longer in the Above, sometimes he will bring a new book back for me. Usually, his long trips result in the gaining of food for us all, a book for me, and something small for my mother, like a leaf or flower that only grows in the cold, bleak conditions. It is a sweet gesture that he loves her, and that her old world is not gone completely.

I guess this lightens the mood quite a bit when you've been staring, hungry, at the same four walls waiting for the return of a family member from a world which is supposedly now dangerous.

Each time my father leaves, I catch a glimpse of blinding whiteness before we are covered again.

"It's closed to protect you," he says about the manhole cover every time, but it is always with slight doubt, as though our staying here is not helping anything.

Everything that keeps us here is to protect us.

Each day is the same.

I wash.

I sharpen the spears my father uses to catch fish from the cold water.

I boil water. And then I boil some more.

I cook our food.

I read book after book after book.

My mother and I are waiting for my father, sitting against the walls on the opposite side of the fire to one another. She yawns, and, out of pure boredom, I mimic her. Each time I get a little louder until there are many echoes, which change from yawns to giggles. It's as if there are thousands of Riley's yawning and laughing aimlessly.

My mother looks up from her book and at me disapprovingly.

"Riley! be quiet. Your father will be back soon." But she is smiling slightly.

I am pretty much her only form of entertainment.

Sighing, I sit back and stare at her from across the room. My mother was once very pretty. She still is, but in an ill sort of way. She is skinny like me, with auburn-brown hair, cut unevenly to her shoulder, and large dark brown eyes. Her skin is pale like mine. There are bags under her eyes which are slightly more noticeable today. I am told by both my parents I look a lot like her, but I have never seen my own reflection. At least, not of which I can remember.

In the evening, the mood dampens.

Sometimes, we will tell stories and laugh and sing. My mother tells beautiful stories. Often about how the Above used to be. But the best stories are those about my brother. He is family, still with us but not really. "With us in our hearts," My mother says.

There are not any stories tonight though. My father isn't here. We are tired. It is dark and cold, and the fire is burning out quickly. It is hard to keep it alight with what little firewood we have left, but we still try.

"Are we gonna stay here for the rest of our lives?" I randomly blurt out, a mixture of sadness and desperation forcing the words.

"What do you mean, Riley?" she says hesitantly, not looking up from her book. Her hands start to shake, but I pretend not to notice.

"This won't be home forever. It can't be. Surely there's a way we can live up there, someh–"

My mother sits up abruptly and looks me in the eye, a gaze full of so much emotion that it overwhelms me. She begins to speak, then stops herself, rewording and rewording again compiled sentences in her mind.

In the end, all she can say is "No, this won't be home forever."

My heart beats a little faster, pounding against my chest at the thought of being up there with nothing but the remnants of the storm. Then she continues, with warning and concern in her voice.

"And when that time comes, you need to protect yourself with every bone in your body." I want to ask a thousand questions, but she looks exhausted, so I let her close her eyes. When she is asleep, I walk over to her and pull the worn blanket up above her shoulders, take the open book off her chest, pop it to the side, and kiss her cheek.

"Goodnight, mum," I whisper so quietly that almost I can't hear myself against the silence.

Chapter Two

Three weeks have passed. We are short on food, short on firewood.

We are short on a thousand different stories told only by him.

Essentially, we are short on everything that fuels us.

He should not have gone so far as that he would put our survival at risk. Even if he had come back after a few hours with merely a handful of winterberries (which is apparently the nearest available food source when he does not travel to the central city), it would have been better than to wait this long.

We both think about my father without stopping to think about anything else. To keep warm, I wear my boots, old and double-knotted, and as many layers as I can find.

My hair messily covers my blushed cheeks as I wait for the fire to intensify.

"Are you hungry, Mum? I think we have a couple tins left. I'll heat one a little if you want," I ask quietly without looking up from my book, absentmindedly thinking that my mother has been quiet the last hour.

No reply.

I glimpse above the pages I am reading, and she is laid on the other side of the fire, fast asleep, a face slightly tear-streaked. I sigh and then carry on reading for a little before she wakes, slowly opening her eyes, which squint even though there's barely any light entering the room.

"Food?" I ask her gently, smiling just a little.

"Food." She agrees, smiling just a little back.

I get up and pass her the tin with a flask of water, but just as I am about to sit down again, she stops everything, silently pleading with me to do the same. It's only a moment before I realise why.

Panting and shallow breathing from the Above. The part of the Above which is *directly* above the manhole cover.

Panting and shallow breathing from more than one person.

"Riley, go to your room now."

"But—"

"Just respect what I am telling you to do and go! Behind the door, now!" I start moving backwards, but as I walk, I stare wide-eyed at the man-hole cover which is being forced open. I can almost see the clouds which seal off the sky, a grim undulating greyness seeping inside. And then I am gone, heart racing, breathing heavy against the door of my room. Behind it, I try not to cry for my mother, and I try even harder as I hear the harsh grip of hands on her arm, I feel the glacial air strangling me.

"That's one of the missing found. I'm glad you agreed to finally tell us where you've been hiding them, James. They could be a serious threat." James?

"Well, I finally realised it's for the protection of our nation." My father, James. But his voice almost isn't his voice. The sound, his, but it sounds emotionless, almost monotone.

Almost.

Apart from a small croak, one which perhaps is not acknowledgeable for any other person.

My mother says nothing.

Nearing footsteps rattle the old, underground floor. I do the only thing I can think to do, my mother's words echoing in my ear, and quietly but swiftly lay down in a painful looking position. The cold of the ground turns my cheeks blue, my hands are outstretched above my head. I take a painstakingly big breath and hold it, until the beat of my heart is so quiet that I question if I still have a pulse.

My father sees me and gasps. He sounds as though he is going to cry, but he remains still.

The other man speaks, his voice ugly. "She's dead?" He begins to walk over to me and I almost wince. Even from a distance, I can feel the malice from his aura tiptoeing across my every bone.

"*Please,* have some respect." My mother cries, and I hear the malicious man stop in his tracks. "Malnourishment. It happened today." My mother is lying, but her acting skills are admirable. "We can't leave her here, we have to take her somewhere, somewhere with flowers, somewhere—"

"She is not going anywhere, ma'am. We are facing a war; burying this citizen is the least of our concerns, especially after her betrayal."

Betrayal?

My mother gulps, but she leaves without a fight as I hear the steady, hard retreating of footsteps against the cold floor. I open my eyes, making sure they are no larger than slits, and see my father turning back and fixing his gaze upon my face. He catches my stare, a look that transforms from agony to relief, and then to urgency, wide-eyed, as if he is asking me to do something. Confusion soars through my blood as he turns away, and when I hear the manhole cover placed back where it had been with a thud, I let out a silent cry, succumbing to shock and exhaustion.

I open my eyes, and it has grown pitch-black. The fire holds only embers and all I can hear is the distant wind from the Above beating down on our ceiling.

I reach out, seeking my mother's comfort and warmth.

She isn't here.

Slowly, I press myself onto one elbow and warily call out to her, my throat dry and sore. Like earlier, there is again no reply. My heart, for a second, seems to stop in my chest.

And then I remember.

Liam's voice echoes through my mind like it always does when worry consumes me. An older version of him, not seven, but twenty-something, telling me to be strong.

"Mum?" my whisper echoes slightly, sounding pathetic, hopelessly waiting for a reply. I know that there is no point in calling her name. I can feel that she still isn't in the room, that she hasn't made it back.

But I try to pursue more desperation and strength in my voice when calling out again, while hopelessly staring at the empty space on the floor where her huddled up sleeping body should be. I do not like the echo of my own voice, I just long for hers, or my fathers. Or for Liam's voice to be real like it once was.

Underneath, it used to be a place of safety. I may have always longed for the day I could breathe the fresh air from the Above, but down here was my family. Down here was warmth and shelter and light from the fire. It was my safe place, because I had people with me whom I loved. Without them, it feels a million miles away from safe. It feels claustrophobic, dark, haunting.

The wind above tries to fight its way in through the cracks, and I hug my knees.

When my fear eventually subsides, it does so only because I become hungry. I look where our food is usually stored. There is less than half a tin of cold beans, and an open tin of apricots which we have been saving. There are also a few tins which previously held food, but now store water that we had boiled to drink.

21

I eat the beans cold, the entire tin of apricots. I slowly drink two tins of water. I heat the second, because I have grown cold, and I pretend the hot water is warm cocoa as I hold my cold fingers delicately around the tin.

The warmth travels into my stomach and provides an ounce of comfort.

When it becomes brighter from the dim daylight that seeps through a crack in the ceiling, I reach out and, forgetting, seek my mother's warmth. When I recollect the previous night, I am about to pull my hand away, but find myself clutching a crumpled note in the palm of my shaking hand. It is filled with her neat handwriting, some lines crossed out, rewritten and then crossed out again; a struggle to collect her rushed thoughts expressed on to merely paper.

For a while, I do not read it. I just take in the shape of the paper and the way the folded white shines slightly in the small amount of light from above. My eyes linger on it blankly, fingers shaking, a meagre attempt to reveal the words.

A lump in my throat builds as each word begins to seep through my eyes and into my mind, drawing a thousand and one emotions out of me. It is titled 'leaving day' and is addressed with my name.

"If this letter has been left in plain sight for you, and you are alone, you need to leave. It's just as dangerous for you now down here as it is above. You don't know it yet, but you are special Riley, and I have known that for a very long time. We needed to hide your strength because it is a threat to them, but it is time for that strength to be used, and I always knew this day would come. If our plan was successful, they will think you are dead for now, and this gives you time. Your father and I have kept much from you the past 15 years, and we are sorry we did so, but we had to protect you. We love you, Ri."

One time, when I was about ten years of age, my father left as he usually would to find food. I tried to run out after him, but he had closed the entrance before I reached it. Rising as he had done to get out, I hit my head on the entrance and my mother had cried out before she held me to her chest, cleaning my wound. She said I had a small concussion. I didn't know what that was at the time, but everything felt dizzy and hurt endlessly and I lay in my mother's arms just waiting for my father to come home and my thoughts to become clear again.

That's sort of how I feel now, staring confused and fearful down at the note which I hold with my shaking hands.

With swift and quiet movement, I stand and grab another blanket. It doesn't suffice against the cold, so I look around the room to locate more firewood. There is only the mass amount of old paperwork on the desk, some of which has fallen to the floor, but it's better than nothing. I begin collecting it, confused by all my father's rushed, handwritten scribbles. One of which is titled: 'Viral control measure. Effective in temperatures 5 Celsius and below.'

I have never read any of my father's paperwork. I never contemplated doing so. Not once have I believed it would make sense to me, and he had always told me that it wasn't interesting, that it was not for me to worry about. He would look at me and smile, "Ri, it's old work stuff. Don't worry about it."

But the smile never reached his eyes.

In this moment, I cannot help myself. There is more paper almost identical to the first I had read, words semantic of viruses and the weather and the United Kingdom and the population of people there.

Then there are others. These don't appear to have my father's handwriting; in fact, it is not handwritten, but professionally typed. On them are numbers.

And around 30 faces.

The people are classified as missing. None of these make sense to me. I have not seen another human face for years other than my parents' and I assumed most, including my brother, died in the storm.

SOLDIER 82. Missing.
SOLDIER 111. Missing.
SOLDIER 112. Missing.

The faces staring back at me look very much alive, and I instantly recognise Liam's picture underneath 'SOLDIER 111'; his young grey eyes how I remembered them, blanketed with fear and innocence. The air around me does not seem to enter my lungs as I realise my brother, who is now over twenty years of age, may not be dead, but in fact, very much alive.

I stop.

On the paper is a young girl, no older than three. She has long wisps of dark brown hair, and large brown eyes like my mother's. Her smile is wider than I have ever seen anyone smile (although that's hardly impossible given the amount of people I have seen) and there is a singular dimple on her left cheek. Her skin is fair but has a healthy glow to it.

My heart stops for a second in my chest as I read the name: *Riley Carter.* It continues: *Unmarked and missing.* The word 'unmarked' is circled in red pen vigorously, so much that the pen almost cuts clean through the paper.

Quickly, I again find myself looking through the other papers, those with the faces, all of which had the word 'missing' indicated by their names.

There are no other names that have the word 'unmarked' alongside them.

Only mine.

My home for the past fifteen years has never seemed so different. I had always known this had been somewhere in which my father came to work privately before the Storm—it would have been next to impossible to just stumble across it to find safety—but these seem far from simply doctor-related notes.

They seem like they are governmental documents, meaning that civilisation still exists in the Above.

It takes a moment before I realise that I've been holding my breath, but even when I breathe again it feels as though no air is entering my lungs.

In the evening, my head rests on the cold ground and I stare at the ceiling blankly, confusion swirling through me like the wind that I can hear hammering above me. The paper on the fire burns quickly and roars just as my stomach roars with newfound hunger, which my mind attempts to ignore. It sparks luminously against the dark of the night.

Then it turns to ash.

Chapter Three

"Please, Mama, I hate it when the darkness comes. Can we not keep the fire burning for a little longer?" I am nuzzled into my mother's chest, and I can feel her heartbeat as she whispers reassuringly into my ear.

"If you let me get rid of the fire, the story I am about to tell you will feel so much more real."

I lift my head, feeling a rush of excitement soar through me.

"A story about the Above?"

"Yes, dear. A story about the Above." She chuckles.

I agree reluctantly and watch as she waters down the very last glowing embers from the fire.

She continues. "When it is dark in the world above us, there are billions of stars in the sky, providing just ounces of brightness from light years away."

"Stars?" I ask curiously.

"Small sparks of light sprinkled into the black sky. If you look above you, you don't have to focus on a single star, and yet, you can see all of them at once."

I wake to something wet tickling my entire face, and I find my head tilting upwards toward the ceiling. Just visible is a small hole, and snow droplets are fighting their way through to me, embracing me with their coolness and foreignness from this outside world that I can barely remember. It feels different and at first, I do not know whether I like the difference or not. But I strangely come to accept it, not resisting the droplets but letting them fall until I can almost smell the air that is pleading to get through.

I push myself up from the ground and begin walking over to my father's desk in the corner of the room. In the old drawers, hidden by layer upon layer of dust, I find flint, a compass, and another tin of fruit. The fruit looks debatable, but I grab it anyway, desperation leaving no exceptions. On the desk lays my mother's note, in the same place I had put it down after reading it, hands shaking. Next to it are the papers with those labelled as 'the missing'. In the drawer there is also a large folded piece of paper. When unfolded, it shows uncountable amounts of overlapping lines. A big blue line runs through the middle which reads 'River Thames'. There are words, places, like 'Kensington', 'Westminster', 'The London Eye'.

A map of the Above. Of London, of home.

Some areas on the map are circled vigorously in red pen. My father has made a key at the top of the page, with red labelled 'training camps'.

There seem to be camps across the country.

After folding away the map, I pull my attention back to the drawers and find a small, ragged rucksack, which I place everything I have found. I put on some of my father's large socks, my boots, double-knotted, my mother's cardigan, a hat, gloves, taking care to prepare myself—physically and mentally—for the cold that I will inevitably experience.

For a long while, I walk around the office-like room, my own room. The place I have lived for fifteen years of my life, where I have built most of my memories. The same four walls that surrounded me, day in and day out. The cooking, the reading and writing, the longing for freedom, the stories of the Above, the fear for when my father was gone, the relief when he returned.

Fifteen years.

The other three years? I have barely any recollection.

I know I cannot stay here, and I have known this unquestionable fact for as long as I can remember.

But now I am alone, I finally have a reason to act on the very fact that has both terrified and excited me my entire life.

Adrenaline provides enough energy for me to lift the chair from my father's desk. I move it directly under the manhole cover and test its weight. It does not break; I weigh seemingly less than a feather.

My hand reaches the cover and lightly pushes against it. To my surprise despite having seen my father do the same thing many times, it easily budges, revealing a small gap at the side. I am not sure what I was expecting, but it feels as though the simple manoeuvre of the cover from the ceiling should have been a lot more challenging than it is.

Still, I can't help thinking that if this is so easy, then I had been meant to leave all along.

White light escapes through and I wince, looking away so I do not fall. I think about a physics book I read once; about how white light contains all the visible colours of the spectrum. I wonder what it is like to embrace all colours, let them absorb into the lenses of my eyes.

I look again, slowly this time, opening my eyes only slightly, and am about to climb out before something runs over the top and pushes me down so that I fall, hard. My cry only lasts for a second before quickly, I am covering my mouth. Whatever it is that ran across now stands next to the cover, its shadow looming and falling through the cracks. Listening closely, I can hear its breathing, which causes my own breathing to stop.

It feels unbearable, after a while, to just lay here and watch. The thing is no longer moving, like a statue, its shadow laying still.

Cautiously, I climb again on to the chair, careful not to make any sudden movements. My hand touches the cover, pushes it to the side. It opens more and more, slow and fast all at once. My heart is racing, all the while light is again seeping through, blinding me. I was right, someone, something sat there, not far from the manhole cover. My heart pumps as though it is trying to escape my body, and I want to run.

But there is nowhere to run.

By the sound of it has steady breathing, I convince myself that whatever lays overhead is resting, which might give me enough time to escape. Grasping onto both sides of the exit, I pull myself up enough so that the top half of my body is no longer underground. I then use the full force of my body weight to lift the rest of me up and over. The air strikes me, cold like ice, but it is fresh, compelling.

And then I see it.

In stories my mother has described them. Her description has manifested itself right here, a surreal sight standing right in front of me. It has large ears, a long black nose, short brown fur and white spots along its back. Suddenly it opens its eyes, large and brown and filled with wonder. They are, I imagine, the mirror image of my own.

I am staring directly into the eyes of a doe.

In this moment, I don't think I remember anything more magical, than to stare in the eyes of an animal I have never seen before. An alive animal, an animal that has survived the Storm.

Very much still breathing, still beautiful.

I first expect myself to run, because this – not just the animal, but 'this', this whole world – is so foreign to me, and I have no idea what to do. Though I may lack knowledge in this new world around me, the doe looks to be little danger.

Once I have fully heaved myself out from underground, I crouch down so I am at her level, making sure I am careful not to overwhelm her. Sitting on the ground that had once been our ceiling, I feel the air, the coolness, the breeze. Inhaling deeply, an overwhelming sense of freedom hits me like nothing I have ever felt.

The light is too blinding for my eyes and everything is now a blur of greens and whites and browns and greys. I try squinting and rubbing my eyes, but it doesn't help.

The doe evermore continues looking at me wide-eyed, and I do the same. Then shortly after she stands and prepares to move away, looking back at me expectantly like she is waiting for me to follow her.

To my astonishment, laughter leaves my mouth, a short burst but laughter all the same.

"I'm sorry," I begin as if I am talking to my mother or father. "I don't understand." My head tilts sideways with confusion as the doe repeats its gesture before running in the direction that she had been facing. Like a child, I long for it to come back, curiosity and desperation filling me abruptly.

"Wait!" I shout, and find myself running after her. My only energy source, the adrenaline coursing through my veins.

My eyes are still adjusting to the world around me. The vibrancy of the light is immensely different to the small, insignificant fire we used for light daily underneath. It is snowing, the flakes a blur as I run, soft on my skin. I appear to be running on a pathway, which is lined with old, flickering lights—lampposts—and grey buildings far in the distance. There are trees, but most are leafless, desolate, and covered in a blanket of white.

I blink a thousand times as I run, trying to absorb the outside world which blurs like a painting.

I'm not sure why I follow the doe, but maybe it's because I have no clear plan otherwise.

I want to find out where my father has taken my mother.

To find Liam.

To find out why I had to be kept hidden for so long.

I have been following the doe for what seems like an eternity before she comes to a sudden halt. She is looking ahead with a strong intensity at something moving fast in the distance.

I can hear it then, the loudness overpowering the faint sound of the wind. My mother has told me stories about these, vehicles that carry you around to places in the Above as if by magic.

Still my eyes are sensitive to the light, but by squinting, I can just make out the silhouette of what by my mother's past descriptions appears to be a train. It's approaching a station in the distance, but from here I cannot make out the exact location, or much of its surrounding area.

For a moment, I look at the doe breathing fast, now within close proximity to me. Her eyes are fixed upon the now visibly decrepit train, which is both eerie and awe-inspiring. I consider how it is as if she has led me here, but quickly brush away the thought with ambivalence, remembering that she is an animal and not a human being.

I take a breath and begin patting the doe's head softly, cautiously, before I begin to walk towards the train, fast, shaking but determined. I walk so quickly that I do not see the tree stump in front of me, or the hole beneath it in which an elderly woman appears to be hiding. Her greying wisps of hair and kind smile are revealed as she begins to walk cautiously towards me, letting the light touch her face. Her hands are fragile, shaking, sleeves pulled right down to her fingertips.

Above all, she is a human.

Very much alive.

I think I need to sit down.

"Oh, dear. Is it safe to come out yet?" I almost jump out of the shock from just hearing another person's voice. Hers is old, kind, fragile. It is hopeful and loving.

My own voice is apparently trapped behind some non-existent wall in my throat.

I look from her to the doe, her to the doe.

"Not the *deer,* she won't understand me. You, dear."

I begin walking away from the train and towards her, retracing my steps with no idea what to expect. My voice doesn't emerge, so instead, I wait for her to continue speaking, to fill the air with words that are not my own.

"So, is it?" She continues with persistence. I am unsure of what to say. I don't *know* the answer to her question. I look at her. The doe still looks longingly ahead, and it takes me a while to see what she had her large eyes fixated on.

Behind the now still train, the other side of the station platform, there is grassland. It is covered in snow, and it looks unhealthy, but there are sure enough masses of grass and trees amongst only few abandoned buildings. In the doe's eyes, there is clear longing for exploration and food. The train is just an obstacle, and the doe has been contemplating whether to cross it or not.

The woman watches me, waiting for a response.

"I'm," I start, my voice small and hoarse, gaze still fixated beyond the train. I cough and try again. "I'm not sure what you are talking about. I'm not from around here."

I walk back toward the train just as I had been walking before, my steps quickening with the women's words echoing in my head. She is a human, very much alive. Yet, still concerned over a threat which I feel I am yet to witness; the danger my father had warned me about.

When I look back with more curiosity than I thought I could behold, any sign of her presence, even a single footprint in the snow, is gone.

Chapter Four

Liam

Among the trees, our fire roars loudly. We all sit around it; any closer and we would surely burn ourselves. Not that we'd notice any pain, because our bodies are far too numb from the cold, blue limbs and frozen fingers we possess.

Despite not being able to feel my fingers, they continue to move as I play my old guitar. Part of me wants to play it as loud as I possibly can; a cacophony reminder to the world around us that we will not willingly conform to their standards. Noah joins in with our small, seemingly insignificant melody, drumming on the old upturned bin. He is always so light-hearted, always has a sense of humour, and you can tell that now, by the slight grin surfacing on his face. But, like me he is still immersed in the music, concentration lingering in our eyes as we escape from everything.

Ebony merely sits glancing over at me, the fire illuminating her small, child-like face. Two dark, messy plaits fall either side of it, and when she looks at me her eyes are partially covered by them as though they are curtains, hiding her from the world.

We found her around a year previously, sat with her mother against an old telephone box, desperately trying to get her attention. Her mother, like most, stared blankly ahead and in no way responded to the cries of her own daughter.

At least, not in a way you'd expect a mother to respond to her daughter. There was no calm, no love, just pure nothingness; an abyss full of empty words controlled by the outside world. She was gone like the rest of them, with just a soulless chunk of metal, a gun, clutched tightly within her grip. The soldier knew of nothing but to attempt what she had been forced to do: kill anyone with a voice.

Ebony wouldn't stop begging, a persistence I have never seen in anyone. She screamed and screamed until her high-pitched voice was reduced to nothing but a whisper, while I forced the gun from her mother and secured her tightly to the telephone box.

Now, Ebony holds onto her soft toy bear tightly against her chest, fearful I will try to take it from her again. I once told her we should not hold on to objects that reveal emotion and expose ourselves as individuals, such as the bear which I reluctantly agreed to let her keep by Noah's persuasion. It is a form of individuality, of weakness, and *they* hate that. I would much rather we didn't get caught, but Noah said it wouldn't benefit anybody to take it away from her. He then laughed and said we'd probably both end up in pieces, while Ebony watched with solely warning in her eyes. The time I had tried to take it away, my arms had scratch marks by her nails from my shoulder to wrist. and I don't intend on receiving them again.

Noah is singing now, his voice slightly hoarse and extremely imperfect. Sometimes it annoys me, but he reaches enough key notes for it to sound bearable.

In fact, the sound is strangely comforting, and my own voice joins, both of us together sounding almost tribal.

'*Keep watch of the eyes watching you.*
Their lungs are filled with ice, their hearts are frozen.
Don't look them in the eye, or else you'll be chosen.
Imagine what it's like brother, to not have a soul.
Looking out of those dead eyes instead of your own.'

Our old hats and scarves are pulled tight as we breathe the harsh cold air of the night.

Around us, it is seemingly peaceful, with only the rhythmic sound of the burning fire and our music, low and instinctive. The ice on the ground reflects the small amount of light the sunset provides, or would provide if there was no mist in the sky. The leafless trees move slightly in the wind, and the buildings in our vision are small, far in the distance. In a way, it feels almost free out here, the music and the wind and us.

Here's the catch. You aren't free in this world.

We are here not to live, or to feel, but to not feel anything at all.

We are here to be controlled.

Something happened that night; the night of the storm.

Something changed everyone.

They no longer have control over their minds. I am not sure they even have anything in the least like a soul. As far as I know—out here at least—It is only us who do: Noah, Ebony and I. We are the missing, renegades, an assemble of trouble and inconvenience for whatever the government have spent years planning.

The sound of a twig breaking forces our music to cease abruptly. Noah and I stop singing, grab our bags and stand as though we are ready to make a fire drill exit, abandoning our own fire which is continuing to burn behind us.

Ebony doesn't move.

"Ebony," I whisper, hurriedly. "Come on." Her reluctance to run is unusual; in fact, her reluctance to listen to us is almost non-existent. It is as though, for just a small moment, she has lost the fight. She stares blankly at the fire, while Noah grabs a hold of her arm and pulls her up lightly.

But then she opens her mouth, small and dry from the cold. And she begins to sing; not to us, but to herself. Her strong accent is quiet but noticeable, her voice wobbling, a tear in her eye. Still, as she stares at the fire behind us while being dragged away and pulled into a run.

"Imagine what it's like, my brother, to not have a soul. Looking out of those dead eyes, instead of your own."

And then we hear it. The screams and calls and knowledge that we are here, about to execute an escape.

"Hey!" They call in unison, a whole bunch of 'em, the searchers. People who look for us, the ones who cannot seem to abide by societal rules simply because we aren't controlled by whatever is in this poisoned air. "Get back here!"

"Over our dead bodies!" I shout into the space behind me, dragging Ebony along. I can feel my nails digging into her small, fragile arms, and her pace is worryingly slow. Noah sees my struggle amid panic, rushes over to us, and hurls Ebony over his shoulder. She watches out for the voices as he runs, her eyes wide and more terrified than I have seen them since she left her mother.

Behind us, the crunching of sticks and the sound of foot against ground quietens with each step we take. The screams are becoming gasps of breath, and their sense of direction is faltering. But we run still, as far as we can run, as quick as we can run.

When we reach what appears to be the safest resting place—hidden in among trees in another area of forest—I can't stop my anger from pouring out of me like water in a sieve.

"Ebony, for God's sake! When…I tell you…we need to leave…we need to leave. You don't…just…damn sit there!" We are all still catching our breath. I hold on to the tree trunk beside me, its coldness merging with my fingers.

"Ah, come on, man, we just took her away from her mother—" begins Noah, and although I know he speaks sense I cut him short, now wanting nothing more than to cast my anger elsewhere.

"Her mum was *gone*, Noah, like the rest of them. Besides, it was a year ago. Shouldn't she be over it by now?"

"No, Liam, she's human."

I immediately regret my words, looking over at the twelve-year-old girl who has known nothing but this world of hostility her whole life. Marked as a soldier the very day she was born out of her mother's womb, still marked when she escaped and tried to rescue her helpless mother with her. 'SOLDIER 100,000'. The 100,000th civilian to be deemed property of the government.

Ebony makes no sound other than the quick-paced breaths which escape her small mouth. Her brown, freckled skin has a slight redness to it; partially because of the cold and partially because we have been running for what seems like an eternity. There is also an almost definite possibility that it's red because she is trying not to cry.

In her arms, she holds tightly on to the soft toy. I look at it, knowing it is not just a soft toy, but it is the only piece of a childhood she will ever know.

I sigh, walk over to her and place a hand on her shoulder. It is my way of silently apologising. She looks up at me with her large dark eyes, and they soften. She rests her small head against me, and I let her stay there for a little while.

Then I study our surroundings.

Around us, there are no more sounds, just endless trees. I can make out the train tracks not far south, but they aren't close enough for us to be seen if we are careful. There is plenty of wood for a fire, and we still have some tins of food in our bags.

"We stay here tonight," I give my order and then walk away, looking for somewhere close enough to them so that I can stay guarded, but far enough so I can also be alone for a while.

I'm sitting high up in the trees, not caring if I fall. I stare down at what is visible of London. In the distance—the buildings, the train tracks—up here everything seems so much closer. It sends a slight chill down my spine as I envision what this place used to look like, and in response I wrap my arms around my chest for a second until I can feel the smoke of the newly made fire warming me from below.

It's not long after that the branches rustle about and my momentary silence is disturbed. Noah discreetly murmurs a sound of pain—which is probably from hitting one of his limbs against the tree—as he climbs on to the branch beside me. For a moment, he just stares ahead as well.

He can't bare the silence.

"You better hope this branch can carry the both of us," I say half-heartedly, eyebrows furrowed against the cold breeze, casually glancing downwards to make sure Ebony is safe.

"Oh, I'm light as a feather. Not so sure about you though." Noah laughs and pats my stomach. I let him do it, reluctant to grin.

I grin anyway.

When we were young, Noah and I had both been standing next to one another in a line of thousands of children whose minds and hearts had been reduced to nothing from the cold.

I was directly in front of him, shaking out of fear and trying to do whatever I could to calm myself. We mimicked those around us. We mimicked their blank stares, expressionless faces. But we could not mimic the dullness in their eyes, so we avoided direct eye contact with anyone we saw.

Although Noah and I were only six and seven years old, we had been smart to have pretended we were one of them. Somehow, we felt the danger that came with not pretending; we should have been like them but were not. Something went wrong in us, wrong for the government anyway. They didn't predict such immunity.

We were marked just as the rest of them were, a unique, permanent tattoo allocating us to the role of 'soldier' in the new world which is not our own. Noah had been marked to a different camp than I, but there was only a twenty-minute train journey from Mayfair to Paddington. Every day at dusk we would meet halfway, away from the camps and in the gardens of old, abandoned homes, planning our escape.

I consider Noah's wrist for a long moment. Still marked, still deemed property and not people. Yet, somehow, we aren't affected; I guess you could say we are freaks of nature.

It may have been ten years since we escaped, but these tattoos on our wrist still hold us to them; the government is tightly latched on to us, whether we accept it or not.

"You know what?" Noah says, bringing me back to the moment high up in the trees, the bitter wind numbing my face. I don't reply but turn to face him, indicating he has my attention.

"They're out there somewhere, the rest of them. There's gonna be more of us. You know, other than your father."

Silence.

After I let his words marinate in the air for about a minute, I say bluntly, "Then I guess you believe Santa Claus exists too, huh?"

"Well, yeah, pretty much. Look around you, there's snow everywhere. It's practically his home." He grins, pats me on the back, and hops down from the tree with a loud thud, followed by another sound of pain.

I follow him, grimly scraping my hands in the process which quickly become red and sore. But before I have a chance to acknowledge the wound that should be there for longer than a moment, I close my eyes. A rush of energy soars from my mind to the wound, which then seals itself and becomes merely a small, insignificant scar.

A freak of nature.

Ebony is laid fast asleep with two of our three thin blankets. I grab the last from my rucksack and hand it to Noah. He rejects it at first, trying to push it back towards me, but he knows I'll refuse to take it from him. So instead, he accepts it and puts yet the final blanket over Ebony to keep her warm, before Noah and I pull out jacket hoods up over our heads, and our scarves around our mouths and noses.

With one more cautious look around our hideout, I quickly fall asleep, taken back to a warm world which no longer exists.

I wake to bitter cold. The fire has completely burnt out, leaving only remnants of grey ash in its place.

My stomach growls. Noah and I exchange a knowing look as we both acknowledge there is no food left. The forest around us doesn't appear to hold any edible food, and we haven't visited a camp to steal substantial food in a long time. My tired eyes regard Noah for a second, and his do the same to me. His cheeks look hollower, and the usual glisten in his stare has faded. There is even a notable paleness to his skin, his natural olive now almost ghost white. From the way he is looking at me, I know I mirror his signs of malnourishment.

"Hey," he whispers tiredly, a painful croaking sound coming from his throat. "Where's Ebony?"

Crap.

"I, I have no—" Before I can finish, I hear her small footsteps getting closer and closer.

And then Ebony is standing directly in front of us. I watch as she proudly presents a handful of fresh, bright looking berries.

Crimson red, like blood.

One bursts in her hand, poison just inches away from her mouth.

"Ebony, STOP!"

She drops them all in a heartbeat. One berry rolls to the bottom of a tree a few metres from us. A tiny squirrel leaps at the opportunity and eats it, before falling to the ground almost instantly after. We stare in unison at its lifeless body. Its head rolls to one side on the snow-covered ground, looking deadly at us without blinking once.

"What were you thinking?" I almost scream, while watching as she falls to her knees and bursts into tears. But despite my anger, I grab her in my arms, feeling more need than ever to protect her small, significant life.

Chapter Five

Riley

I am fearful, of course I am. Almost the entirety of my life has been spent hiding underground with just my parents for comfort, for company. The ground feels as though it is shaking, the doe still debating whether to run to the other side of the ever-moving train.

The train is slowing to a standstill.

No, Riley, come on. Have strength. This might be your only way out.

Quickly, but only momentarily, I turn back, but there is nowhere else to go. No alternative, no better option. I see the manhole cover, the tree where the old woman had been, and the white nothingness far behind me.

I want to have hope, but I am by no means giving off hopeful energy. I am emitting waves of distress, and they are flooding everywhere around me. I imagine my fear like an avalanche, rushing faster with every beat, beat, beat of my heart.

Snow blankets the floor. Around me, the world appears different to how I had envisioned it, or perhaps to what I remember from the small years of my life that I had spent here. I would think the Above – the city – is deserted, had it not been for the old woman, the wildlife, the train. It is abandoned, desolate, devoid of the warmth that had made it worthwhile before. Like my surroundings, it is as though time is frozen, a picture frame with no people inside it.

I continue to walk, adrenaline fuelling my every step. My eyes widen and fear strikes me like a dagger, fast and lingering. I think at first it is the woman behind me, pulling me back. My scream escapes me, muffled and hoarse. I turn around abruptly and consider the eyes of a more than familiar face.

The absence of life is replaced by my father, who gestures for me to hide. Without thinking I do as I am told just as I always had done underneath, crouching down behind a large tree, waiting until he sits beside me. He is wearing all white, a sterile outfit which blends into the snow, depicting a surreal image in front of me. His stubble which, had been there the last time I saw him, is now fully shaven, and he seems less pale, but his eyes are equally as tired. I don't know if I am imagining it, but he seems to appear less undernourished and raw-boned.

"Riley."

"Dad…"

"That scarf," he gestures with a shaking hand to the scarf pulled loosely around my mouth and nose to warm my face.

"Have you removed that scarf since you have been here?"

Confusion fills me for a second as I raise an eyebrow and nod hesitantly, before pulling the scarf away from my mouth to speak.

"Yes. Dad, what's going on? Where's mum?"

He ignores my questions, his eyes filled with apprehension. "DON'T! Don't breathe in the air. Just in case we were wrong."

"I'm fine. Don't you think, if the *air* was going to damage me, it would have done so by now?" Despite saying this, I subconsciously raise my fingertips, covering them gently over my lips and nose for a small moment. When I am confident that I in no way feel different, I remove them, take a breath of the striking, cold air, and consider my father. He is looking at me not just as though I am his daughter, but as though I am a fundamental entity, the missing piece of a very important puzzle.

My father surveys our surroundings, and I follow his gaze, squinting so that everything blurs a little less.

"I don't have long before they realise that I'm gone, Ri," he stammers a little in his words, a weakness present which I do not think I have ever heard from him, before pleading "Listen to every word I say."

And so, I listen.

"When you were born, a war launched upon the Above – upon Britain. We did not have a big enough army to overthrow our opposers, so the government asked a group of biomedical scientists to devise an artificial virus; one which would attack the minds of our entire population and force them to conform, becoming a part of one unstoppable army. The last virus model, to me, was an implosion; it only breeds in the cold, and more importantly, takes away everything in our minds that makes us fundamentally human. Now, our biggest enemy is ourselves. But that's where you come in."

I stare at him wide-eyed in disbelief. "Where I come in?"

"When the virus was released, not everyone could become infected. Those with the strongest minds… their ability to think and act for themselves remained."

"The missing…" My heart stops inside my chest as I envision Liam's small, childlike face staring back at me from the coarse paper file.

He continues, leaving no room for me to process my emotions.

"Your mind is the strongest. You are a threat and—"

I stop him in his tracks, an overpowering sense of anger finally catching up with me.

"How can I trust you?" I demand, reluctant to back down even when he tries to stop me. "You made this. You made all of this," I gesture around me towards the desolate city, not caring if anyone or anything sees me. "And you seriously expect me to trust you just because you protected me for fifteen years?"

"I didn't know it was going to be like this, but you needed protecting; you weren't ready to face them, Ri." I used to adore how he called me Ri; the short but sweet nickname was a constant reminder that he was protecting me. But as I look at him now, James Carter, I remember nothing but the cold, hard work he put into each day, the work that would contribute to a very different world than the one I once knew.

I don't know who he is anymore.

"I don't care if you *think* I am special. I am no more special than you or anyone. I will not trust whatever plan or instructions you may have for me, and I do not need you to protect me."

"Riley—"

He sounds sterner, but I cut him short, refusing to give in to the pain in my chest, or the tears that are trying to fight their way out of my eyes. I bite my lip hard to keep myself from crying and repeat in a firm whisper "I do *not* need you to protect me."

I turn away from him and look up. Through the clouds I can make out a pinprick of light emerging. If I close my eyes and let the light cover my eyelids, I can almost envision the pinks and violets and oranges of a sunset far behind the clouds.

I remember reading once how the observable universe is around ninety-two billion light years in diameter. I'm not entirely sure what that means, but I like the sound of it, the way it's so limitless and no object, no being, no star is completely the same. The universe isn't observable at all now; fog limits its visibility, as if the sky had never even existed.

"Please, Riley." My father pleads for my attention again, a hopeless last attempt to make me listen. But I can already see it, my escape, a decrepit piece of metal which somehow races through the wind relentlessly.

And then I am running.

His shouts pierce through my ears as I run, his steps fast at first, but to my surprise nowhere near as fast as my own.

The train appears closer and closer; soon I can decipher the back-carriage door which appears to be loose on its hinges, and this stirs my determination even more.

My legs ache and I am struggling for oxygen, but this kind of tiredness is not the sort that you can rest for. It is the tiredness that is told to be quiet by the river of adrenaline flooding through you.

My feet travel at a speed that, having lived underground most of my life, I had never known possible. They run willingly despite the sweat pouring from my face, despite the racing thoughts questioning if I should have stayed. I can feel the proximity of the train, barely an arm's length away from me. I reach out but the cold metal skims my fingertips, refusing to let me reach it.

Come on, Riley. I beg to myself desperately. *Come* on!

Reaching out again, my hand grasps the door handle, and I am pulling myself up onto a small ledge just in front of it. For a moment, a small ounce of pride soars through me. But then my pride is taken away in all its entirety as I look into the distance, squinting my eyes. Without thinking, I hold out one arm while still clutching the door handle with the other. I stretch as far as I can, stretching on the edge of impossibility, hanging off the ledge, trying to confirm what I am seeing. Maybe I am hallucinating from a lack of oxygen? Or maybe he really is there, had managed to catch up so that he now sits in the middle of the tracks, crying into his knees regretfully. Maybe I am imagining it, or maybe he really is screaming the words "What have I done?"

"You lied to me..." I whisper into the wind, knowing that he cannot hear me.

I had fooled myself into thinking I was brave, that I could formulate a plan. But now, as I weep silently into the harsh cold air, brave is the furthest thing from what I feel.

Liam

We walk in silence, making no noise other than the quiet shuffle of feet through snow. We walk until the number of trees begins to decline rapidly, indicating we are leaving the forest's safety. But none of us have a choice. Food is scarce; we either die out here or die trying to survive. I prefer the latter.

A river not far South of where we are heading proves warm enough to bathe. A thin layer of ice on top easily breaks when Noah throws a rock at it, and so we trudge in one at a time, fully clothed, reluctantly allowing the water to embrace us. It turns our bodies bluer than the sky's blue, back when the sun shone and we could see clearly without a permanent stretch of grey and white clouding our view.

Into our flasks, I fill more water while the others dry themselves. The exhaustion in Noah's face is clear and distressing; the way his eyes are bloodshot, his mouth dry and peeling. Yet he is determined to make Ebony smile. She is one of us, immune to whatever it is that filled the air and never left it. And he sees her as a sister, concern filling his face every time she catches his eyes. I can't help but feel a sense of responsibility, like we need to protect her because she is a small part of what is left of humanity.

After we have bathed, Ebony sits watching Noah throw snowballs into the water aimlessly, but she is struggling to smile. Noah is sighing, giving up with his newly acquired role of big-brother-makes-little-sister-laugh. Instead, he takes on the role of big-brother-attempts-to-comfort-little-sister, tucking her in with a blanket as you would a small child. I often wonder how Noah has so much love to give in a world that seems to have no love left to offer in return. I let that thought stand over me like a dark cloud and fade away into the darkness, knuckles clenched in a never-ending fear, ready to wake instantly if danger approaches.

I awake to the sound of train on tracks, screeching to a halt. In the dark of the previous night, we must have missed how close it was. It's now roughly quarter of a mile ahead of us, more than close enough to acknowledge its presence. It moves determinedly through the wind, and then it is still. The silence is almost deafening.

These trains carry people on long distances. They carry the people who are gone. We can walk away right now, back in the opposite direction where we came.

But this very train that has stopped within walking distance from us will almost certainly contain food. In my peripheral vision, I see Noah rubbing his eyes as he wakes from sleep, and they are no less bloodshot than before. He begins to follow my gaze towards the train, and I wait patiently for his eyes to adjust.

He speaks now, a voice slow and cautious, yet trying to bring some form of light-heartedness. I raise my eyebrows in preparation for his protest.

"Liam, my friend, my brother. If you're thinking what I think you're thinking…" he is laughing, hoping I'm not being serious.

I am.

"It's a death trap."

He's probably right.

"Oh, for goodness bloody sake."

I hold Noah's gaze sternly. He looks away first, either defeated or perhaps knowing we have no other choice.

I speak with authority, making it clear that I need to be heard. "Okay Noah, you and Ebony need to keep watch when I am on that train. If anyone other than me gets off there, you stay still, you stare straight ahead. Pretend like you are one of them, you hear me?"

Ebony nods silently, fearful but willing. I figure she'll be fine. Noah, however, appears to be contemplating something in his mind. Shortly after he looks as though he has decided something, and I wait for his reply as he inwardly picks his words with endless thought. This means he will try to negotiate with me, and I am way too short-tempered for any of his crap.

"I'm going to have to stop you there," I say before he can open his mouth to talk.

"I haven't even said a word."

"Doesn't mean I haven't seen that face before."

He continues regardless. "If you're going, there's no way on earth that we are just gonna stay here and watch your pretty little face as you go aboard that train. What do you think we are going to do if anything happens to you?"

"Better one of us then all of us."

"Not really, Liam, because if one of us dies the rest of us will sooner or later." This time it's him unwavering, stubborn in his decision. I figure negotiation is better than not going ahead with the plan, and we can't afford to waste any more time standing around and deciding which of us should go ahead. So, we all begin walking, then sprinting across the frosty ground. Our energy is dropping rapidly, and I silently pray that neither of us will faint before we have even reached the train.

But then, almost as if the world is working against us and wholly determined to leave us starving in some woodland area on the outskirts of London, the sound of train on tracks starts again. Noah's speed increases despite myself knowing that his entire body is fatigued beyond imagine, like my own. But my focus is not on speed, not on getting to the train. And that isn't at all because I have given up, or that I no longer have the adrenaline to fuel me. It's not what determines my persistent cries to Noah to keep moving without us, even though he has turned to see what has happened, pure horror and worry filling his face. For a moment I can see how much he wants to stop as I have done, but he is already too far ahead of me and he realises this within moments.

I have let Noah run alone, because I hear human body collide with the ground, cushioned in frost.

Ebony lays there, her head facing towards the sky, eyes closed. Two dark, messy plaits either side of her. Arms stretched outwards; her soft toy bear a few feet away from her hands. Not once had she said she was feeling faint, or that she could no longer go on, that she would wait behind. She never spoke, she just tried to help. She ran with us even though she no longer had the strength to run.

Yet, I failed to hear her silent cries of exhaustion.

Ebony is weaker than the both of us, and I feel so stupid for not noticing that. If I had left her for the train, I never would have forgiven myself. It's easier to survive when it is just me and Noah, but in this frozen moment with Ebony laying hopelessly on the ground, I decide she is our family, our sister. I will not leave her.

And Noah is our only hope.

Chapter Six

Riley

I am bound by exhaustion, but the train is too fast for me to close my eyes and sleep; I must keep awake to hold on, but I can no longer feel my hands as they clutch the rail of the ledge. The cold intensifies and I pull my jacket hood above my head, tying the strings from it into a knot and letting my hair cover my cheeks.

I look at my hands still clutching the railing; I forgot I was wearing my mother's gloves. Seeing them makes me feel a pang of sadness, a longing for her comfort. In this moment, a small part of me wants to be back underground, listening to the stories of the Above and holding curiosity without being here.

I miss them.

But this thought quickly dissipates as I remember how much I want to understand the world, and to understand myself.

The screech of train on tracks is making my head pound. I feel like the train myself, heavy with the weight of my rucksack, the harsh pull of gravity forcing me down.

Slowly and with a painful amount of effort, I stand up on the small ledge, shifting my focus carefully so that I don't slip.

Then I notice it.

Behind me, on the train's outer wall, there is a window. At first, it is hard to see through, as the cold air has coated it with a thin layer of frost. But it is easy to wipe away; the thin layer falls to the train ledge as my hand rubs across it. It's clear enough to see through, so my face presses against the hard, glacial glass.

My heart is hammering against my chest.

Oh my god.

There are people...Excitement and hope overwhelm me as I watch them; perhaps survivors of the storm, the missing? Maybe this means that we are heading somewhere with food and safety and shelter from the cold, to others who can protect us. Maybe society is recovering with the union of the missing, all those who came to no harm from whatever lives in the air. With the last of my energy, I pound against the window as hard as I can using my free arm, desperation for them to hear me, to somehow help me inside.

I need them to hear me and they can't. They don't even blink.

I'm not prepared to give up. In my rucksack, I pull out the flask which contains only a small amount of water left. It'll be louder against the window than my own hands.

I try to convey my desperation as I hit the window again and again. I am clinging on to hope and I won't let it leave. The second time the window is hit there is no response from the people inside, but it is far more forceful than the first time. I close my eyes, inhale strongly the ice-cold air, hold the flask back, and then fling it at the window.

For a moment time stops.

The flask has impacted the glass so that a small crack has formed. It is not big at first, but it begins to grow. And it grows painfully slow, the crack stretching across the entire window at all angles and the bitter sound of shattering pierces my ears.

Everyone on the train slowly turns their head, almost in sync with the sound of glass breaking, and they look me in the eye. I want to say something, but the words catch in my throat and all I can do is stare back, wide-eyed, into eyes which seem so dead.

Am I fabricating the cloudy whiteness of their glares, the paleness of their skin? They all look so ill, yet, these people are clearly alive and moving. They do not once get up to help me or speak to one another about what is happening. Instead, they flatly repeat a string of words which sound so lifeless. A chorus of, "You are immune, you are weak, you will not save us."

I guess they aren't the missing after all.

Quickly, I sit back down on the ledge so they cannot see me through the window. Nothing but panic is filling me as I try to think about what to do.

"Crap."

My panic seems to amplify as fast as it had arrived. In the distance, I can see someone sprinting towards the vehicle as fast as they can, a clear desperation shown by the surreal pace at which they run. After witnessing the people on the train who seem so different to my family, so dehumanised, I should feel cautious

46

and fearful of this person. But somehow, I am not. Somehow, as I watch him jump and grab the side of the train with such force, hear him murmur 'ow' under his breath, I am not fearful at all.

He is just an arm's length away from me, and appears to hear the chorus of voices on the train only once he has jumped onto it, which comes as no surprise in consideration of the fact the wind from the train's movement deadened my own hearing.

A few seconds pass before he looks at me, does a double take, and then his green eyes are full of pure confusion and hope and joy and fear and everything in between.

"Crap, I must've hit my head hard," he mutters while rubbing his eyes with his free arm almost effortlessly, as if it is every day that he jumps onto a fast-moving train.

I say the only word I can think of saying, "Hello."

To my surprise, he simply chuckles a little, revealing a small dimple on his left cheek. But after a split second his face is serious again and I wonder if I had been imagining his laugh.

The train carries on moving, the chorus of people inside the train becomes louder, and my body—as I'm sure is the same for the male next to me—aches beyond belief.

But no words surface in the depths of my mind other than a simple introduction in a not so simple scenario, and now I am slightly embarrassed.

"Now isn't *really* the time for introductions, I'm afraid," he shouts through the wind, his voice light-hearted but serious, focused, all at the once. "Stay here just one second?"

Before I can answer, before I can beg him not to leave, he has already climbed over to the back of the train, nudging me gently to the side. He looks at the window, then his eyes dart around until he catches sight of my rucksack. He grabs the first item his hand encounters—my water flask—and let's go as he flung it as the window.

"I'd duck if I were you," he shouts across the wind; the crack I had made earlier now disappears altogether as the glass seems to fly in the air, both behind us and inside the train. He pulls himself through the window and runs across the train carriage, avoiding the seemingly lifeless monologue that is still being recited: "You are immune, you are weak, you will not save us."

I can't help but gasp, my heart pounding against my chest as I watch this male grab what looks like canned food from closed compartments around the train, throwing them into his own rucksack while at the same time avoiding the outreached arms of the crowd. I should still be ducking—glass continues to elapse around me, and if I'm not careful I'll end up injured—but I can't help myself, I need to watch him, to make sure he is okay.

"Oh my God…" I shout through the wind, realising my personal dictionary appears to have decayed into only those three words.

He ducks underneath the arms of an older man with eyes as blank as the snow. In that instant, an alarm is now sounding through the entire train, and I think I might faint from absolute panic but then he is out, heaving himself up out of the window and back onto the ledge on the back of the train, his face close enough to mine that I can feel the warmth of his breath on my cheeks.

"Hello," he smiles despite the alarm and the people now slowly walking towards the window, the rush of wind and the sound of the train, the chaos of it all. "Sorry about the delay. I'm Noah, and you are?"

"Erm, Riley."

"Hi, Riley. Now, in an older world I wouldn't have usually asked someone to jump off a train when first introducing myself, especially because of the dangerous risks that come with the former activity. However, right now it's the best option we have and I'm going to need you to trust me. Will you do that?" Any words that I could have replied seem to be stuck in the back of my throat.

"Okay, good," he says, as though I had replied to his insanity. Noah suddenly grabs my hand and before I can say another word, he jumps and pulls me with him. As we lift ourselves from the ledge, I am floating, everything blurred in a swirl of white.

And then, everything goes black.

Chapter Seven

Riley

The first thing I feel is an unbelievable pounding on my right arm. With my good arm, I reach over and touch it, coming instantly into contact with a layer of material. I am no longer wearing my jacket, but instead, it is placed like a blanket on the left side of my body and most of my right side, other than my arm which lays flat on the cold ground beside me. After pushing myself up and attempting to force my eyelids open, the damage to my arm becomes evident; redness has seeped through the layer of fabric that has been tied tightly around it. Before I begin to feel queasy from the sight of it, I direct my attention away from the injury and instead to my surroundings.

I am laid behind a frozen-over bush, and there is not much else directly in front of me. If I look far ahead, I can just about make out the train tracks in the distance. Seeing them makes my heart pound with fear.

The sky is dark, but there is an ounce of light and I think that it is either dusk or dawn; I can't decide which. Behind me, a far distance away, I can just about see many small dots of light illuminating what I guess is an assortment of buildings from the city's centre.

Confusion overwhelms me, and I settle down again only to find my head laying on a bundled-up coat that is not my own.

Then I remember. Noah and the train and the dead-eyed people.

For a moment, I just stay still and feel oddly comforted by the quietness and ounce of light both in the sky and in the far distance. But the quiet gradually looms over me in a much less comforting way, and I want to know where Noah is, where I am.

This time, I do not slowly sit up, but stubbornly I stand against the pain and throw off the coat that was laid on me. Wincing, I put my injured arm through the other sleeve of my cardigan and look around. Sitting directly opposite me in the darkness, just looking ahead, is what looks like the silhouette and eyes of a young girl. Somehow, I am reminded of blank stares on the train and memories of before flood back. The young girl's stare, however, is not like there's. It is not blank, but it is hard to comprehend what exactly she is feeling. At least I know she *is* feeling.

Cautious, I walk backwards, forgetting about the bush that had been beside me as I fall through it and land on my right arm, heaving in pain.

"Careful," the girl inhales, a quiet but somewhat strong voice that I can only just hear. She gestures towards my arm. "I bandaged that up for you." She has a bandage around her own head, perhaps from a fall, and small scars cover her youthful skin. I am not sure what to say, so I say nothing, just staring at her wide-eyed with inquisitiveness.

Then comes another voice, male and familiar. "I was starting to get worried, Riley, it's been forty-eight hours since you've been out. You must be parched." There is genuine concern in his voice, but there is also a joyful buoyancy that makes me want to smile. He holds a flask with his outstretched arm, which smells like warm cocoa and bubbles up with froth. I take it immediately, cherishing every drop.

"Noah?" I whisper questionably. I sit up straight and, without thinking, poke his shoulder with my good arm. He tilts his head to one side and raises an eyebrow. "Sorry it's just…you are real. Wait…am I hallucinating? I've read somewhere you can hallucinate pretty bad if you hit your head. I did once when I had a concussion. I hallucinated that I was here in the Above," I can't stop myself; I am word vomiting everything swirling around my brain all at once, and it is making no sense.

"The Above?" He questions at once, intrigued. I just gesture around me, before he begins to chuckle. "You aren't hallucinating, I promise, Riley."

"So, you really are Noah?"

"That would be me. This here is Ebony, and Liam's over there by the fire." I exhale a sigh of relief that he is here, and not like the people on the train. But my attention is pulled instantly towards Liam. He has dark hair and pale skin, and his eyes are a similar grey to my father's.

It's a coincidence, I think to myself, as I look away. I am certain I had hit my head when we jumped from the train, but the undeniable, instinctive feeling in my mind is difficult to ignore. He shares the same name, a similar appearance to my father. Yet, I conclude that if this male is my brother, he will have noticed me as much as I have noticed him.

The rest of the day consists of Ebony silently offering to aid to my injuries Liam ignoring me, and Noah repeatedly passing me food and water from what he had collected on the train. I am too tired to ask any of the many questions that shoot back and forth repeatedly in my mind, so I just lay back and watch the grey sky, feeling the air's mist and snow embracing my entire body.

Every so often I drift off into sleep, dreaming of deer and the old woman, fear and snow, my father and my mother, blank stares of the people who, quite frankly, I believed were dead. I dream of a storm; the sudden cold during summer, a season which I barely have recollection of.

Between dreams I eat a little in silence, and in my peripheral vision through my tired eyes I can see Noah's concern and other unreadable emotions, sensing that he himself has questions to ask me.

Later in the evening, when everyone else has fallen into a deep sleep themselves, I dream what I am sure is not a dream but a memory. A memory that I can't remember storing somewhere in my mind, but a memory that confuses me, further inducing a tiredness that refuses to leave.

I am three years old again; I know because I am in our old house, and everything is here. Our family portrait, with Liam reluctantly accepting a huge hug from me, a small smile creeping upon his face. My mother and father, both smiling down at us, hands on our shoulders protectively. The television is on, the news, and my father is watching it intensely from the coffee table as I sit cross-legged on the floor.

Liam is watching too.

The news presenter looks at the camera with eyes fearful and dark, and it feels as though he is looking directly at me. His eyes tell the story of someone who doesn't want to remain calm like a presenter must, but instead shake everyone's shoulders and scream with terror.

"Another day, another death. Seven more people have been named dead from yesterday's bombings, released from what police are saying is yet another declaration of proposed war. Our hearts have been crushed yet again by the losses received. The question everyone's asking is this: Do we have the strength to fight back?"

My father's phone rings, and I can feel my small heart pounding against my chest. He answers and all he can say is "yes, I am coming now," before he grabs his jacket and leaves in urgency. Tears roll out of my eyes as the door slams, but Liam jumps off his chair at the table and runs over to me to make me laugh; a small 7-year-old who somehow knows exactly what to do to take care of an even smaller 3-year-old.

The scene changes then, abruptly, and we are standing among many buildings, directly opposite what surprisingly I remember to be called the London Eye.

Momentarily, a rush of excitement soars through my three-year old self as I look up in awe and wonder at the big wheel.

But that quickly dissipates.

"Oh god," my father whispers. My mother picks me up in her arms, surveying everything around her while she grips me and Liam tightly.

Snow is pulsating down on us, a harsh cold blanket.

Something in the air feels different, as though my lungs are being filled with a drug. I feel scared, but nothing else happens to me.

My father looks around as though he is searching for something, someone.

Then he looks at Liam and I, a full force of worry filling his every bone. "I know somewhere they won't find you; we need to go now okay?" It's not a question, but an order. Liam and I are pulled along; me in my mother's arms and him clutching her hand.

I look past her shoulder and see that Liam has lost grip of her hand. He is on the floor, crying out to my mother silently.

She can't hear him.

If her hands are like mine, she can't feel them because of the cold. The hand that was holding Liam's is still in the shape that it was when it was wrapped safely around his own.

"MAMA," I scream, but there is wind so loud I can't see Liam anymore.

"MAMA, get Liam!" And I hit her and hit her on her back as she carries me, but we are numb and cannot feel anything, and she won't look back, but she keeps looking forward and running and running and running.

There is pain right in my stomach, and it cries for my big brother, for home. Everything hurts.

I wake up screaming, my breath looking cloudy in the cold air.

Liam and Ebony are fast asleep, and on the other side of the fire in the dark of who knows what night since I have been here. My eyes widen from the trauma of the dream.

I look at Liam then, older and taller but undoubtedly sharing similarities with *my* Liam. The same hair, the same thoughtful crease above his eyebrows, the same tenseness while sleeping, as though preparing for an attack.

My brother.

Maybe it's just a coincidence, I tell myself despite the knowledge flowing through me that this person is undoubtedly, inevitably my big brother, who, before finding my father's files, I thought had been dead.

Tears once again begin to fall down my cheeks as I wonder if a time will ever come that there is no longer crying, but only laughter and happiness.

Probably not anytime soon.

"Psst, hey, crying never helped anybody." I had forgotten Noah was awake and jump slightly as I pull my gaze away from Liam to look at him instead Somehow his eyes, tired and bloodshot, tell me what he is going to say before the words even reach his lips.

"You got enough energy to talk?"

It takes half an hour or so, but Noah has soon collected enough firewood to make another, smaller fire some distance away from where the others are laid, so as not to wake them.

I am sitting, hands tucking my knees to my chest, silently wishing the flames will quickly build up and warm my body. Once they have, he sits opposite me and I am shocked as, for an instant, even Noah doesn't know what to say. Still, it is not long before he finds his words.

"So, Riley, I understand this is all weird to you." He pauses, smiles a little, expectantly waiting to see if I will say anything, but I just wait for him to continue.

"I thought we could just talk. Because you look like you have some underlying questions you want to ask yourself. You know, maybe like: 'Why is this guy so funny and handsome?' Or perhaps you're thinking, 'When will he shut up?' I don't know, Riley, take your pick." I start laughing then, an unexpected snort, but laughter all the same. I am embarrassed, but he smiles with me, revealing small lines under his green eyes.

"See, there we go." His smile is warmer than the fire. "Hey, why don't you go first? Maybe you'll answer some of my questions when you're asking your own."

"Well, erm…" I don't know what to say for a long while, but Noah sits patiently waiting. How can I even try to communicate the fact that I had no idea anyone else was alive on this earth, that I was made to believe I and the rest of my family were the only survivors.

Clearly, this is not the case.

Instead, I gesture to his wrist and ask, "What's that?" There, on his scarred skin, appears to be an imprinted word and number. 'SOLDIER 112.'

"Wait, don't you…" he is looking at my wrists. I reluctantly pull up both my sleeves, and he inspects them as though I should have a similar mark imprinted on me.

He is momentarily shocked, and begins to ask, "Where have you…" but he stops short. Maybe he can see the confusion stamped across my face.

Then he seems to realise, seems to remember something.

Before he can continue, I counter ask, "What do the numbers mean? On your wrist?"

"It's our number in line, when we were marked." He pauses. "You know those people on the train we saw, the ones looking dead, but they were quite clearly alive? When me and Liam were kids, we were in a line among hundreds, thousands of these people. We tried to act the same as them, imitate their blank stares and lack of emotion. One by one, we all walked towards these people. They were dressed in like, masks, lab coats, I don't know, I can't really remember a lot more about the way they looked. But when it was our turn, they tattooed our wrists, a word and our number in line."

I look at Noah with dismay, wondering what to say exactly. Him answering one question has not settled my mind, it has stimulated it, and now I can't think straight as my brain becomes a point of investigation, an adjure for further elaboration.

He speaks again, and I can tell he isn't used to being the serious one. But maybe he knows now is not the time for too much levity. "You see, they have camps for these people. We for years continued to mimic their blankness. Liam was in the clearing next to my own, training to fight. I was training to defend. I heard those in charge were trying to find the missing. You and I, by the way, we are the missing. It is probably only us who are, considering no one else would try to escape; they are completely submissive, completely controlled."

"No," I say quickly as I think of faces I had seen on the paper underneath, back in our home, just days ago. "There are more, I'm sure there are more." I look for my rucksack so I can show him, but I see it in the distance, back with Liam and Ebony.

Noah holds my gaze and nods slowly, but it's clear he doesn't believe me.

"I hope there are more," he says.

We both pause, quietly watching the flickering lights in the distance.

"Noah?" I breathe quietly.

"Riley."

"Why did all this happen?"

The distant lights stare silently back at us against the mountain of white. I think they are buildings. Maybe they are the camps, and the gone are there, and the missing people, the people like us, are elsewhere.

Maybe the missing are watching the lights too.

"Now that isn't a question for me," he replies cautiously. "You'd need to ask Dr James Carter."

Noah

"I don't understand what's so special about her," Liam had asked when we first arrived, watching with hurt as she slept.

"You're sure it's her?" I asked him, looking at her as well.

"Yeah."

"They didn't leave you behind because she's more special, Liam. You know it was an accident, the strength of the storm."

He had ignored me, walked away as the memories flashed through his eyes, a montage of flashbacks to his mother losing grip of his hand. He still hasn't spoken to Riley since she got here. Not once.

In this light, her eyes have this kind of gold ring in them. I am looking at them reflecting her surroundings, and I'm thinking how she kinda looks like her brother, all apart from her eyes.

Why am I so fixated on her eyes? They're just eyes, for God's sake.

Back to the task at hand: Try and explain to her what is going on—well, at least, how much I know is going on—while finding out how much she does *not* know. Her head is facing the ground when she says it, and I am sad, because her golden-brown eyes should get to witness all the colours, not just absolute whiteness from all the frost.

Riley

"James Carter is my father," I sigh, without looking up.

I wait expectantly for a sign of shock in Noah's face, but he holds only understanding. I think it's understanding at least, because he has the sort of face that is always somewhat unreadable, even when he is smiling. He nods while tucking a strand of matted brown hair behind his ear and looks down towards the floor.

"I know," is all he says.

"You know?"

"Yes, Riley. I know." He smiles then, just a little. "You're Liam's sister. He told me while you were knocked out from your fall." He isn't asking me this, he is telling me. Just announcing it here and now.

I sit for a moment, a long moment of comprehension. Or little comprehension. Or no comprehension. Liam knows I am his sister and has not said anything to me during the entire time of which I have been trying to work out if he is or not.

After a while, Noah chuckles and asks what I am doing, and I realise that I have been staring straight at him absentmindedly without saying a single word. He is now examining my face, looking for revelation to exactly how I feel. But I myself don't know exactly how I feel. Am I shocked that he knows I am Liam's sister? Shocked that Liam knows I am his sister? I am a book of interrogatives, and the pages know no bounds.

"Thinking," I reply, slowly. For a moment, I sit in silence, letting the eerie atmosphere wrap its hands around me.

"Have you spoken to my father?" I find myself asking.

Many of the distant building's lights have turned off. The lights are gradually being replaced with abstracted noise of who knows what. I am coming to my own silent conclusion that the buildings are the camps that were listed on my father's map.

"Yes, but not since we escaped camp." says Noah, his bright eyes continuing to penetrate through my skin. They are like how I imagine the ocean to be; big and scary and beautiful. I feel a weird sensation in my stomach when I force myself to look at him, but I shyly look back again at the floor and stare a hole into it.

"Doctor Carter, your father, he supposedly works for the government."

"Supposedly?" I ask, an ounce of hope that he is innocent starting to creep back into my heart. With it comes guilt, the consideration that maybe I should have trusted his plan, whatever that had been.

"I trust he is actually working against them. Trying to build a new army to reverse the mess he helped create."

I search his eyes for lies, but they are bursting with sincerity.

"If you trust my father, then why are you no longer with him?"

Noah sighs, and as he does so, the green in his eyes seems just a little less luminous.

"He may have wanted to build an army, but as far as I know, there isn't enough of us. This virus he made, it's too strong. No point us being there."

He stops, long and contemplative. I can feel him watching me. In my peripheral vision, I anticipate the warmth which seizes me. It is welcoming, so I look up completely, allowing it to fully consume me.

The black sky has lightened into a grey mist, and a new light falling of snow covers the floor. I feel as suffocated as the ground, trapped in a white layer of lies and confusion.

"He found me up here, tried to make me come with him. Apparently, I have some kinda strength, but I couldn't trust him Noah, not after all of this."

He doesn't speak, just nods silently. A gesture of understanding, as if he'd seen it before. I consider that maybe it was the same with Liam. Noah seems to understand the life story I am yet to tell him, even though I have only just met him.

Not that there is much to understand.

"Why isn't he happy to see me?" I gesture towards Liam in the near distance, who even sleeps apprehensively. His fists are clenched as though he will be attacked any moment now.

"He thinks he was purposely left behind. Because he isn't special, isn't what Father needed to protect."

"That's ridiculous. He is just as immune to whatever is in this air as I am." I stand. Although I don't want to believe it, the possibility of what Liam has proposed to Noah makes my blood boil. I imagine my mother and father being completely aware of Liam having fallen in the storm, not stopping to save him. Around me, the wind becomes more chaotic, stirring my anger and drumming the trees with each beat of my heart.

"Riley," Noah places a hand on my shoulder, and a sense of calm flows like a river through my blood. "It was an accident, okay."

"Okay." I breathe, feeling the wind come to a halt around me.

I spend the next few days trying to convince Liam I am not in any way special.

To make him trust me.

A newfound stubbornness prevails in me as I mirror what my brother does, trying desperately to help find food, light the fire, rebuild shelter from old branches and soil. Repeatedly though, my attempts often fail. The fire does not light, or lights too quickly. The shelter falls instantly or falls later when we are about to sleep, and each time I try to smile at Liam, but he sighs and starts rebuilding. Each time I fail to do any one of these tasks, Noah smirks though, revealing a singular dimple on his left cheek. It's difficult to feel angry at him, because he means well, and his smile is infectious.

I am a sucker for his smile.

He is kind.

Yet, Liam does not smile. Instead, my endless attempts at getting my brother to happily acknowledge my existence grow long and exhausting. The faint memories of how my brother had been do not compare to how he is now.

Liam

It is her.

For that, there is no doubt in my mind. Her freckles are in exactly the same places that they were when she was three, she has the same goofy smile, the same eyes that she shares with our mother.

Noah wanders over, vibrant and knowing. Knowing exactly what I am thinking as I watch Riley pick up firewood heavier than her body weight, drop it, and then pick it back up again.

"You still don't wanna talk to her, huh?"

I shrug. "She's Riley, sure enough."

Noah glances over me, a confused glaze in his eyes. "So, you don't want to talk to her because?"

"Because if I can't trust my own father, how can I trust someone who has been with him for so long."

I sigh. "She's one of us. I don't need proof of that, and you shouldn't either."

Chapter Eight

Riley

Ebony is sat across from me. Her small chin is resting in her hand and she seems a little sad, but mostly bored. Her eyes flicker every time the wind blows her dark hair into them, and she taps her grazed knees continuously.

Beside her lays a small bag filled with bandage and other medical supplies; the same ones she used to tend to my arm. I wonder how long she has been medically trained, where she learnt it. It only now becomes clear to me how she never really says a word, just sometimes smiles.

This girl, perhaps around twelve years old, seems to just make it from point A to point B each day, aiding our wounds and helping to cook. Doing everything she can in her heart to remain loyal to the people who saved her. She is a child and she should be filled with curiosity and life, but she is only filled with dedication and silence.

This is not how it should be.

It is saddening.

I feel my heart pull against my chest as I watch her hug the soft bear in her arms and stare aimlessly ahead. I wonder what she has been through, and where her family are.

Are they dead?

Are they gone?

I unlatch my rucksack and look inside, desperate to find something that might bring a beam of light to her face. My hand brushes over a book, and hope fills me, light and infinite. It is a little damaged but it is still there and in one piece, a montage of colours and illustrations. I walk to her, slowly closing the gap between us, and her head tilts so that she is looking at the book clasped between my fingertips. There in her gaze is the first glimmer of curiosity, and I decide I am going to do the most I can to make it grow immeasurably.

"I used to read a lot, you know, before I met you guys. This one was my favourite when I was little. You want to read?" She takes it and looks at the pages. Although she isn't smiling with her mouth, I can see a hint of happiness as she turns each page, the colour reflecting from her dark eyes.

While she is immersed in a fiction world less scary than her own, I look down at the frost and light snow all around us. Vague memories of snowball fights with my mother quickly surface in my mind. Or perhaps it is a false memory, manifested from the winter books I have read underneath. Whichever it is, I begin attempting to make snowballs, with the small amount of snow there is, in the palm of my hand (though most crumble in unsuccessful attempt) as Ebony watches me. Her usual sad, absent stare has been replaced by what I can only describe as a look of bewilderment, perhaps at how bad my snowball making skills are. Each one crumbles in my fingertips, snow falling hopelessly to the ground.

"Here," she whispers, the first time she has spoken since she tended to my wounds. I had forgotten how she held a clear accent, maybe of African origin. She picks up a hand full of snow delicately, moulding it into a perfectly sized ball shape. "In camp, my mother and I used to have snow fights when we were in hiding, before..."

"Before what?" I ask it serenely, trying to not add force to my words.

"She became like the rest of them. They found she was immune. I hid, and they injected her with something stronger, a mutation perhaps. I escaped the camp and took her with me, tried to save her, but I couldn't. That's when Liam and Noah found me, just a few days after."

She doesn't look up when she speaks, but her dark eyes hold memories which aid her snowball making concentration. There is also sadness.

"You couldn't do anything, Ebony. It's not your fault."

She shrugs, but her cheek is tear stained. Droplets fall into the snowball she is currently forming, marking them with sorrow.

"Have you always lived in the Above?" the words leave my mouth before I acknowledge what I have asked.

"The Above?" she asks, humour masking her face.

"Sorry. Here, in the city."

She answers with a one-worded response. "Yes." Instantly, I feel cruel for reminding her that she has known no different for the entirety of her life.

But she smiles delicately, as though maybe someday she will want to carry on the conversation.

With that smile, she is pretty, she is youthful. She is in a light that I have not seen her in the few days that I have known her.

Quickly, we duck behind a tree trunk just wide enough to cover the both of us, and her smile widens into a large, goofy grin. We hear the ever-growing footsteps of Noah and Liam, presumably carrying more wood for our fire.

At first, I silently debate whether what we are about to do is a good idea, but Ebony's small smile has evolved into contagious, quiet laughter, and I refuse to take that away from her.

Suddenly, she stands and throws the ball swiftly and in a singular movement.

I peer over the trunk to see Noah's shoulder covered by the remnants of the snowball, turning with a face full of confusion. When he sees us and hears Ebony's laughter, his face is filled with both shock and amusement.

Expectation that Liam is angry hits me—purely because of his focus on carrying the firewood—but he only holds disappointment on his face and tuts.

And maybe.

Maybe I can see a small speck of love. Smaller than how a star looks in the sky.

But stars only look small.

They're underrated.

Chapter Nine

Riley

I take a moment to shed the sleep from my brain and distinguish between my dreams and reality. At first, I am unsure if I'm underneath or above, but the light against my eyelids reminds me of the world I had fallen asleep in. The morning is cold and my blanket is thin, but I pull it above my face anyway. I groan as a light wind blows at the blanket, the breeze sneaking under to reach my cheeks. The wind isn't just moving the blanket. I hear something fluttering in, then I feel it against my stomach. I am laying on my back, head rested on my rucksack, and on my stomach sits the note.

Above it there is a small rock, seemingly to stop it from escaping me.

Sitting up, I let my eyes adjust to the dim light and open the note. The writing is messy, carefree, an encompassment of spontaneity.

Riley

As you know, we usually try to hide our footsteps once they are made. Just in case, you know, anyone finds us. But being the risky individual that I am (don't tell your brother) I have left them there just for you to follow. There's a place I think you'll like, and I want you to come see it. Don't leave me hangin'.

– N.

I smile and look up to see his footprints leading away from my feet, and soon after I find my feet tracing his; the soft marks made by his own boots.

I walk through masses of trees, walk around bends, all the while my boot laces trail on the ground. I begin to see the building lights in the distance beginning to switch off, one by one, in time for morning. Previously, I had remarked how the lights stay on all night when I arrived here, and it makes me wonder if the people there ever stop what they are doing, ever sleep. This thought accompanies me while I trudge along in the snow, but slowly travels to the back of my mind as I look around and begin to see the number of trees decreasing slightly.

Entering my vision is a huge amount of water and floating ice; a river which doesn't appear to have a start or a finish.

I pull out the map from my backpack and locate the long blue line stretching across the entirety of London, the River Thames.

As soon as I reach the end of the footprints, which embellish the frosted grass, I pull my attention away from endless river.

His footprints stop at what looks like a metal structure, and suddenly I feel an overwhelming sense of stupidity as I realise how unobservant I had been. When I stand back slightly and tilt my head up, I can see it in full. I am at the side-end of a huge Ferris wheel, which carries slightly iced-over seats filling the entire circumference of my vision. There is another note taped to the end of it.

Climb in.

Trust me.

And so, I do.

I am probably irrational, stupid, insane. But still, I heave myself up on to the lowest hanging chair and sit very still for a moment.

That moment is gone within seconds. Suddenly, there is a jolt, and the chair begins to move, creaking as it does so.

I am moving upwards.

Another jolt and Noah have jumped in beside me, a large, lopsided smirk filling his face as he watches my wide eyes and listens to my fast, panicked breathing.

"Did you get my note?" He asks, regardless of evidently knowing the answer.

"Of course, I got it. You practically fastened it to my stomach." I didn't intend for this to be funny, but he chuckles anyway. His laugh is intriguing, and I could listen to it all day, so I hate myself for interrupting it.

"Um, Noah?"

"Yes."

"What exactly is happening right now?"

"Just wait."

"Is it saf—"

"Riley, is it too much to ask that you trust me for a moment?" he says softly, tone far more assuring than his words. "Hey, I know, just close your eyes."

I do. I close them and focus on my breathing and let the cool, early morning air wash over my face while gripping the sides of the hanging chair.

Then when he nudges me, I open them.

I can see the world. Okay, maybe not the world. But I can see…London? Home.

There are many, many trees and the buildings are separated among small, fragmented areas, with the train tracks leading to and from each. The huge, winding river sparkles as though it is made from a thousand stars. From my mother's old stories, and from books, I recall the Big Ben, which does not seem to be ticking. Instead, its hands are frozen. Time itself is frozen, and I want this moment to last forever.

Ahead of me the sky's like I have never seen it; it is red and orange and pink and bright and beautiful, and I breathe everything in, holding my arms out by my side and feeling my smile not just on the surface of my face but inside of me completely.

The wheel keeps turning and when we arrive to the ground again, any colour in the sky no longer visible. I question whether what I saw was real or a figment of my imagination, while Noah jumps off, runs somewhere, and there is soon after another jolt, stopping all movement.

Silently, I beg him to make it go around again, just so I can be up high and feel the cool air from above.

Instead, he runs back, offers me his hand, and pulls me out of the chair, before we collapse underneath it.

"Is that what it feels like to be alive?" I breathe, speaking my internal thoughts aloud.

"You haven't seen anything yet. This world may be broken, Riley, but it doesn't mean everything within it is broken. I just wanted you to know that." He pauses. "Also, I enjoy taking risks and Liam hates that, so I kinda wanted someone to share it with."

I laugh. "The Above – this world – is already dangerous, and you want to add to that danger by sitting in a creaking Ferris wheel that probably has not been used since everything happened. Are you insane or just completely irresponsible?"

"I don't know," he smiles, looking up towards the sky.

"Probably both."

For a moment, I am silent.

But suddenly my mind races, a million and one questions flowing through me uncontrollably.

"Noah?"

"Yes, Riley?"

"I don't understand why this had to happen." I gesture around us, not at the beauty of it, but at the absence of humanity.

Noah almost looks as though my words are his own, but his had been locked behind iron bars for so long. It is as though by me asking his own question, the iron bars have bent and adjusted, freeing what had been held inside for so long. I admire for a moment the way his eyes light up, maybe because he feels just a little less alone.

But he seems to understand little more than I do.

"People do crazy things to win war, Riley."

As the words leave his mouth, I am reminded of the people I had seen on the train. The way their eyes were devoid of anything human. I feel a tight knot forming in my stomach. Noah, one last thing—for today, anyway—what do you think makes a human, well, human?"

He pauses for a very long time. I can feel myself going red at the possibility that he thinks I am some weird philosophical maniac, but it doesn't take long to realise he is simply thinking by his furrowed brows and creased forehead. He is in such deep thought that he doesn't even attempt to blow away the long strand of matted, light brown hair that falls in front of his eyelids.

"What makes us human? The unexplainable, overwhelming, beautiful and innate ability to be anyone we want to be. Uniqueness. No one is the same. We all have different beliefs." He pauses. "Well, we did. And that, I think, was beautiful."

I look at him and know within my heart at this moment what else I find inexplicably, undeniably beautiful.

The written notes and following of footprints in the early hours of the morning seem to have become a regular part of my routine, as is the rapid heart rate that accompanies it.

Each morning, we walk to the London Eye.

Our campsite has become settled for a while—Liam says we are safe and have no need for travel yet—so I have memorised the way, but I still enjoy tracing Noah's footsteps, prominent in the frost-blanketed ground.

This morning the note is tucked in my left palm; my fingers intentionally placed to keep it clasped there.

Riley,

No London Eye today, I'm afraid. I thought we could go somewhere else.

You might have to look a little closer. This place isn't exactly right in front of your eyes (see what I did there? You know, because London eye...okay, okay, I can already see the look of disappointment on your face. But I mean let us hope you're laughing too—that was the intention.)

— N.

I do have a look of disappointment *and* I am laughing; it bewilders me that he knew this before I even knew it would happen myself.

As always, I am careful not to wake Ebony or Liam. We have settled our campsite in a large, plant-filled area, like a large sheltered bush, so I must duck underneath the overlaying branches and watch that the soles of my boots do not crush the old tree bark. To my surprise, it seems like only seconds before I reach the end of Noah's footprints.

I'm confused.

I have reached masses of trees, but there is no Noah to be seen. Nor is there another note placed anywhere.

I recollect his note.

You might have to look a little closer. This place isn't exactly right in front of your eyes.

I look again at the ground to check I haven't missed anything, and that's when I see another footprint, only half-visible. By lifting the branches that seem to cover the other half, more footprints are revealed, almost like the branches are a hidden doorway. I crawl under, and then I see him standing there on a large mound of ice, with what appears to be makeshift ice skates on his feet. They are formed from his own boots, with a sharp layer of wood underneath as the blades. To attach it, it appears he has partly frozen his shoes so that the ice acts as a form of cohesion.

This man does not seize to surprise me. Not once.

He holds out another, smaller pair of makeshift ice skates, and I wonder where the shoes he used have come from.

"Size four and a half, right?" he questions jokingly.

"I find it concerning that you know my exact shoe size."

"I find it weird how you know the size of your shoes when it is the least of our concerns in this world."

"I think you don't realise how much spare time I've had."

There is a short pause, where we both briefly look at each other in slight awkwardness.

Then Noah smiles. "Anyway, I didn't know the exact size of your feet. These are some of Ebony's shoes. They are a little big for her, her being twelve and all, so I figured I would make use of 'em elsewhere."

I try not to laugh at him, funny and stupid and confident as he is. Instead, to stop myself bursting into what seems an inevitable bout of laughter, I attempt to distract myself with the world around us, the Above; everything broken, yet somehow beautiful. The persistent winter weather, bitterly cold on your skin, but everything so open.

Or the gone, who were once unique, now all just the same. But still, they are there, still a part of this world. I still believe there is good, and part of that goodness is right here in front of me in our own makeshift skating rink.

I succumb to laughter.

After I carefully put my skates on, Noah reaches out his arm and tells me to hold on. Then quickly, the whole world is spinning around us; a glittering white globe with its problems blurring from view. It is cold but warmth somehow fills my stomach and I don't think I stop laughing until we fall backwards, heads tilted towards the early morning sky which spins from our vertigo.

When I eventually catch my breath, I look down towards my feet, and the ice glimpses in my eyesight. Reflected there are Noah and I, our faces a mixture of exhaustion and thought.

I cannot remember the last time I saw my reflection.

The longer I look, the more I see my mother's face in my own. Her dark hair, large eyes, skinny body but somehow beautiful all the same.

Tears flood my eyes rapidly, uncontrollably, inevitably, but before I can hide them Noah nudges me softly with his elbow and smiles. I am bewildered and flushed with understanding when he whispers, "She'll be okay," knowing I am thinking of my mother.

I look up at him.

Noah

In the dim light, her eyes are circled with golden rings and wonder. They are huge and fixating and everything all at once. I don't think I've ever seen someone still so…so seemingly curious, so hopeful.

I mean, I guess there's technically only me, Liam and Ebony, but still. I've never really considered whether I'm hopeful or not. I just try and bring levity to the situation whenever I can.

Her long hair blows in front of her face, and she quickly pushes it behind her ear, blushing as the cold hits her cheeks. I find myself looking down, probably because I can feel redness flushing my own cheeks.

Great.

Riley

"I have something for you," he says, softly. He reaches underneath his scarf and unlatches something from around his neck.

"This was my mother's." His expression is more serious than I have ever seen it as he sits beside me on the frozen grass. "It's a St Christopher." I smile a little, looking at the delicate, rose-gold pendant. My cheeks are flushing, and I'm glad they were already red from the cold before. "Also, this matches your eyes." He moves behind me and gently attaches the pendant around my neck. I look down at it, my once bare neck now decorated with something so small and beautiful.

He continues, a glimmer in his eyes. "It's probably an old wives' tale, but, ya know, they're supposed to keep you safe. I've been wearing it for a while but I think it'll suit you better."

"I'm glad you are my friend, Noah."

For what seems like forever, he is silent, eyes full of comprehension, face unreadable.

"Yeah," he says. "I'm glad about that too." He smiles, but it doesn't quite reach the depths of his eyes. Quickly though, as if he doesn't want me to see this, he pulls me into a hug. His arms are warm and protective, and his face is kind and I stay there without saying a word.

Chapter Ten

Riley

"Riley?" Ebony is sitting next to me, speaking between mouthfuls of the edible berries we are eating for breakfast.

Noah and Liam left early to gather resources, with Liam insisting that Ebony and I spend a day to rest. I look at her and smile, secretly feeling valued by the fact she has spoken more words to me since I have been here then she has apparently spoken to Noah and Liam.

"Yes?" I answer, smiling at her. She smiles back, clumsily spilling berry juice down her chin from between her teeth.

"Do you think we could make a boat and go to Japan? I could find my family and my people, and they can look after us. Maybe they can come here and help find my mother." She looks at me expectantly, dark eyes wide and hopeful.

"You have family in Japan, huh?" I wonder how she knows her origins, having only known a mother that succumbed to the world's control.

She shrugs, a small smirk creeping upon her face.

"They have computers in the camps. I managed to do some research, when they weren't looking. I taught myself how to speak Japanese, too." She pauses, pondering over how to say her next words.

"It's, actually what allowed me to escape with my mother."

"Japanese?" I ask her.

Her dark eyes hold mine with an unshakeable grip, and she smiles a small, devious smile. "It put them in a sort of trance when I spoke it to them. I begged them to let us go in Japanese, looked them in their eyes. '行かせて'; 'let us go', and they did."

"I..." My words get caught in my throat. I want to believe her, but I feel as though I am suffocating in a storm of ethereal phenomena.

71

"I can show you," she whispers audaciously. I think about how my father had mentioned those who were immune, who had strengths.

"I…"

"Riley, Ebony, hope you are both well rested!" Noah paces into our area, a huge grin surfacing upon his face.

"Ebony," I say shyly, not looking into her eyes. "You asked if we could get to Japan, find your family?" She immediately loses the light in her eyes and remembers our initial conversation.

Her head faces the ground hopelessly as she says, "It's not possible, is it." It isn't a question, but a statement.

"Maybe we can still help your mother." I smile. Noah looks at the both of us curiously, and Liam mirrors him, standing just a few metres away.

"You really think we can?"

Liam looks over to me with warning in his eyes, urging me not to give Ebony false hope. I look back at him daringly as I reply to her "I don't see why not."

She smiles and I make a mental note to carry on our conversation when we are alone again. Whatever abnormal strength she possesses, *if* she possesses it, may help me to understand why my parents had kept me hidden for 15 years.

The note this morning is tucked behind my long, mangled hair; it blows slightly in the breeze that is picking up fast. The air does not feel as fresh, not as exciting today. It feels eerie, colder, and for the first time since I have been at the Above, I want to be back underneath, huddled up next to my parents.

Silently, I remind myself that the people are around me are just as much my family, and despite the lack of shelter they are my comfort.

Ignoring the disconcerting feeling that grows fast within me, I pray with my eyes squeezed shut, lashes growing frost coated.

Afterwards, I push myself from the ground and look around.

Noah is gone, as always.

But so are Liam and Ebony.

In the distance, I hear the cries of desperation calling Noah's name, and suddenly realise I have overslept, and that Noah is likely to still be waiting for me, wherever he is.

My heart does not sink as much as I thought it would at the idea of Liam and Ebony finding out our secret morning routine, which had somehow become a magic of sorts to me. Instead, I feel a surprising sense of panic from my intuition, and do not expect the same desperate cries of '*Noah!*' to escape my own lips as I rush out from under the blanket.

Liam runs over to me and begins to shout.

"Riley! Where is he? Where is Noah?" He grabs my shoulders and starts shaking me, shouting in my face not cruelly, just panicked, desperate. Ebony just stands from a distance, watching, frightened, dark eyes unblinking.

"Where is he, Riley? Do you know?"

It takes me a moment to find my words, fear all-encompassing despite the sure hope he will simply be waiting for me as always, a Noah-style lopsided smile on his face.

Right?

"It's okay, I know…"

Words stop.

Noah's footprints are followed by another set of footprints, far too big to be either Liam's or Ebony's. Still, I gesture towards them and force a small amount of false hope, "Well, you already know where they are…right? You've followed his footprints…you know—"

"No." Liam pulls his hand through his hair, his eyebrows creased, beads of sweat somehow filling his forehead despite the cold. "We followed both sets of footprints. He is not there." And with that, Liam opens my hand and presses a note into it. I open the scrunched note slowly, reluctantly.

Your immunity is dangerous to our survival.

The handwriting is not Noah's.

A single tear rolls down Ebony's fearful face. She walks up to me as I sink to the floor, taking me in her arms and accepting my sobs. In my peripheral vision I can feel Liam watching, his unspoken words the epitome of disappointment, not of his sister but of himself, for failing to protect his friend. His brother.

And then he is here, holding us.

For the first time.

Embracing his sisters.

Noah

My smile fades.
That is not Riley.
Crap.

Chapter Eleven

James

The government feared their own people's safety because we were all different. Different ethnicities, different races, different beliefs and views and loves and hates. Such difference means rebellion, it means a lack in the number of those who will fight, who will win the war for us.

So, what did I help the government do?

Build a kingdom where those differences are eliminated. A world where everyone thinks the same, so that we will all fight back with no opposition.

But it shouldn't be this way.

We aren't fighting for our people's survival anymore. We are fighting for the survival of robots. They look as people look, but they are not the people they once were.

Our biggest enemy now, is ourselves.

I reach into my lab coat. In my hand, I pull out the photo.

My family.

They are smiling.

They are together.

In a world before the one I helped create.

Suddenly, guards burst into my door grasping a hold of Noah, a boy who I have not seen in so long, now a young man who tries not to look me in the eye.

"Noah Jordan, Dr Carter. We found him, and it appears the virus is no longer effective on him—if it ever had been at all." The guard looks at me almost accusingly, and I pray to God that I am imagining it.

I do not look at Noah either, for fear my face will indicate that he was always immune, and I have always been aware of this.

"Okay," is all I can say, slowly, desperately trying to figure out what to do.

He doesn't look at me, and I do the same; it isn't exactly hard to draw my attention to the room around me. I have no doubt it was here among other places that the majority of lives were transformed into practically artificial life. Not long ago had Liam and I been in these grounds, but not once have I been where the falsity was created.

I always liked James, but now, seeing him in this laboratory, I can feel Liam's distrust surfacing within me. I understand completely why we left, put our lives at even more risk, just so we no longer had to play along to the government's game.

We were sick of surviving.

We wanted to live.

Right now, I should be showing Riley how to live. Letting her make me laugh unfailingly.

She encapsulates the old world in fullness.

Her curiosity towards the world is beautiful. Sure, she is scared, and she misses her family and I feel the exact same. But she still sees beauty in a place so cruel and twisted.

I feel a small, unexpected smile surfacing on my face at the thought of her, but it is quickly dissipated as I am hit hard in the stomach by the man who found me while I was waiting for Riley. The striking pain overwhelms me, and it's almost as though it radiates towards James because he winces. Twice. I take a deep breath and feel calm flow through my veins, like a river.

The man looks down at me, in response to my smile. "You think this is funny, do ya, kid? Well, that's the wrong response."

It takes all my strength to look up at him, but I look at him anyway; he is grey-eyed and dressed in full white. "Sorry, I forgot that no response is the best response. For the protection of humanity, right? Whatever that is anymore." He kicks me this time, harder, and I would have fallen to the floor if it wasn't for his firm grip on my jacket by the cuff of my neck.

This time James speaks.

"STOP…just, stop, okay. This is not for you to deal with. I'll handle it. I'll investigate. Just, just leave the young man with me, okay. Are we not supposed to be *finishing* this war?" It was not a request, but an order, and I am bewildered when they just drop me and walk away, closing the door behind them. So obedient. So dull.

It is though they are gone too.

A few moments pass before James helps me up and leans me against the wall.

"You've grown," he says quietly, sitting next to me while clutching his lab coat around him even though it is far from cold within these walls. Close up, I can see he has circles around his eyes, bloodshot with new lines underneath them. He is not malnourished by any means, but his eyes are more faded than I have ever seen them. Finally, after the pain from my stomach subsides, I respond to him. "I know, I'm surprised too, given the lack of food I have eaten." I say this to bring levity to the conversation, but it ends up sounding almost accusatory, as though Liam's voice echoes within mine.

"Is Liam safe?" he asks, ignoring my comment, to which I guess I am secretly glad.

"Yeah. I mean, he was before I got taken here. Oh, and James."

"Yes?"

"You know Riley's with us too, right?"

At the mention of his only daughter's name, his eyes light up a little. He seems surprised and relieved, but he doesn't say anything.

"Did your wife—Emelia—did she leave your home too?" Instead of answering my question, his face is sadder and less wilful than I have ever seen it, turning towards the window and locking eyes with the blank ones of a woman. She is beautiful, or was maybe, before her eyes were turned into a misty abyss of nothingness. She reminds me of Riley, but without the liveliness. She stands among others, who raise their arms in unison. They are holding weapons.

"Why haven't you helped her? You have the authority to do something, James."

He looks at me dejectedly. "I assumed she would be immune, like our children. I assumed she might be special. But as soon as the air hit reached her lungs..." He pauses, clears his throat. "Do you know where exactly Riley is? And Liam?"

"We built shelter, but I was blindfolded the whole way here. I couldn't navigate us to them if I tried."

He sighs. "I need them. I need all of you."

As if by impulse, I look down at my wrist.

'SOLDIER 112'

Through my mind, I recall our time here, following the orders of others with as blank a stare as we could force upon our faces. Using weapons to shoot targets. Believing it was defence made obedient by this virus that everyone else was under the spell of.

But I realise we weren't just training to protect our people. We were training to fight.

To kill.

To become as bad as those who started the war.

I look up at James, straight into his grey eyes. I consider the heavy bags underneath them, the colour draining from his face. All that is left is but an ounce of hope.

"I don't understand what makes us of so much importance, Riley of so much importance, in winning this war," I whisper.

He takes a breath, inhales so deeply that I am almost afraid the poison in the air will somehow reach his immune lungs. "That's because you haven't seen what you are capable of. You are all more than just immune, Noah."

In my mind, I feel the flickering of a memory. Liam and I, and James too. Liam and I just children, in a large, securely built room. Electrodes placed upon our small scalps, James writing hastily in a notebook, observing our behaviour, our actions. And then, just like that, the memory is gone, replaced by a bout of amnesia. I am aware there is something I am forgetting, something important, but I cannot fathom the exact event.

Instead of trying to recall what happened, I search James' eyes and acknowledge, without a doubt, he knows more about the missing, about us, than we know about ourselves.

"Noah, I need you to help me. We don't have much time."

"Always happy to undo what others have done, James. What do you need?" But I'm serious.

I want to help him more than anything.

I forgive him, and somehow, I trust him.

"To make these people, people again."

Footsteps are approaching the door loud and fast, and I stand automatically, stare ahead, unblinking. James reaches into his desk and grasps a syringe, oozing with a fluid. "A mutation of the virus, more powerful." he whispers under his breath, but without injecting me. Instead, he presses the syringe and lets the fluid fall into a flask, before placing it in his pocket. Following this, he grabs a clean needle, piercing my skin so that just a pinprick of blood begins trickling down my arm.

A façade.

Still looking forward and without moving anything but my lips, I say under my breath, "You're damn lucky I'm a good actor. Just like old times, hm?"

"Not for long, kid. Not for long."

Chapter Twelve

Riley

It is snowing heavily, and our footprints are prominent in the white ground, but Liam doesn't ask us to wipe them away anymore. It's as though we want to be found. We want our tears to be seen.

Ebony walks up from behind me and grabs my hand, looking up with her large, dark, questioning eyes. "Noah is our people too. We will fight for him."

"We don't have weapons," Liam says from in front of us.

"No," Ebony stops, and I do too, my hand still clasped around hers. Liam stops without turning around.

"Then how do you suggest we fight?" He asks, sternly.

"We have something they do not have."

"And that is?"

"Our souls."

'That's…weak, stupid…" Liam says, but as he turns, he is smiling. It doesn't quite reach his eyes, a fake smile at best, but a smile all the same.

He begins to walk again, but it doesn't take him long to stop in his tracks. Ebony lets go of my hand and walks toward an old door, the entrance to a huge building. She pulls a note from it and I read it silently in my head, his hand writing telling me I'd love it here, that he spent ages trying to find it, that he'd always dreamt of coming here and he thought I would too.

I had told Liam coming here—a new place Noah wanted to lead me to— might allow me to find any indication of where Noah had been taken. But now, standing outside this building, I am not so sure. All I feel is a hole in my heart, large and gaping and longing; the absence of his presence.

And fear. I feel fear.

The fear does not stop my feet as they lead me, step by step, into the building, leaving the others to wait outside patiently.

There are chairs, hundreds of chairs. It is dark, dusty, but the stage in the centre has wear which tells stories.

A stadium? A concert hall?

It is eerily quiet, but a singular light shines upon a small object on a chair near the front of the stage. As I approach, I see there are two headphone sets, one which has clearly been used.

My hand shakes as it enters the light, grasps the headphones, places them around my head.

They fit perfectly.

Is this…is this music? My eyes close, and suddenly the hall lights up. It is full of colour and sound, the pounding of drums, the echo of guitars, the freedom of dance and the stories that the words tell in songs of people. He has put songs on here, on this technology, for me, so I can imagine what is like to be in a concert with music from the old world, the Above that I had read about, that I had loved.

The music is my external heartbeat.

It's everything.

When I open my eyes, I fall back and gasp, eyes burning with silent tears.

"Are you okay?" Liam calls from outside.

"I, uh, yeah…just give me a bit longer." I look around me, bringing myself out of the trance and wiping away the tears rolling down my cheeks.

Across the room is a doe.

The same doe from before.

I blink twice. She blinks back, a mirror image, before beginning to run. "Wait, ah crap wait!" I run through the maze of chairs, tripping twice, before I reach it.

"Hello, dear." A voice comes from the back row of seats where the deer stands next to a woman. I recognise her. She sits calmly, smiling up at me, old and tired but bright eyed.

"How long have you been in here?" I respond, hesitant.

"Since the boy was here, and then taken, if that's what you mean." she chuckles."

My heart stops.

"And you didn't help him? You just… you just watched?" More tears begin to roll down my cheeks. Everything begins to spin, and so I grasp the stage in front of me, but it seems to rattle.

"No. I didn't, I am afraid." She looks at me, dares to challenge me in some way. I feel a burst of anger power through my veins.

The ground begins to shake.

"Riley?!" Liam shouts from outside the building, but I ignore his cries. He runs in with Ebony but cannot hear their footsteps above the pounding of my heart within my ears. Snow from outside begins to punch through the building; the doors slam against the wall with every thump of my heart, until they unclasp at their latches and fall to the ground.

"You didn't help an innocent person, you watched as they took him? Who *are* you!?" I scream.

The ground is shaking.

"I am like you. A missing person, immune. Some of us are special, and you, my dear, are special."

I take a breath, clasp my chest which is heaving with pain.

"I am *not* special." I cry.

"Just look around you."

I take a breath, open my eyes, turning to face the entirety of my surroundings. The entire stadium is upturned; it is a sight of destruction.

Liam is staring straight into my eyes, fearful.

Terrified.

Ebony stands next to him, clutching his hand tightly.

"The storm?"

The old woman shakes her head, a small smile creeping upon her face.

"You."

Ebony walks over to me, lets go of Liam's hand to his dismay.

"She made you angry, and then your emotion, it…" But she doesn't continue. Instead, she hugs me, nuzzles her head into my chest."

In this moment, I do not know what fills me more. Resentment? Humour? Hope? Fear? Perhaps the fear shows most, because the woman looks at me and says, "Fear isn't bad dear. It is another sign we are human. Use that. Oh, and they went Eastwards. You'll see the huge block of buildings, and it will be colder as you get closer. The direction they headed is where this weather is coming from." Suddenly, I understand she is trying to help us.

To help me understand what I had been capable of, all this time.

Liam and Ebony do not even question me as I run straight past them, a newfound burst of energy fuelling me. Instead, they run too, strong. Not in physical strength, but in a strength, I don't think any of us knew we had.

Noah

Guards run in, claiming they heard about the lost-now-found rebel soldier, but James stops them in their tracks, holding me by the shoulder as I stare aimlessly at the wall. He holds up syringe, empty all but an ounce of remaining liquid.

"He's no longer immune. Now please, get back to work." They do not answer back to him, just walk away. Part of me thinks it's because they feel bad for James; his eyes are tired, and he looks more drained than I have ever seen him. But the rest of me knows they don't question his orders simply because that is all they know; all they have ever known.

"Come with me," he says while watching the door, just in case they are still listening. We walk, but I have no idea where we are going.

With every step, the air seems to grow colder. The wind picks up, and it takes all my strength not to put my hand over my face to shield it from the piercing weather. I can remember the day of the storm, the day all of this began. It is as though the strength of the storm is back, and we are willingly walking towards it.

It's as though my family are walking away from me all over again.

"James—" I whisper, but he stops me, and I don't persist despite the fact I have no freaking idea where we are going.

Eventually, we reach a tower. It looks as though a hurricane is swirling around it, and it's perfectly clear that this is where the cold is coming from.

James gulps and puts his hand over his face for a second, reminding me of Liam, before he looks at me with a thousand different emotions, but mainly, he is making sure I am listening intently.

I listen.

"I helped develop this virus. The people up there," he pauses to gesture towards the top of the building, "helped to create the machine that manipulates the weather so the virus can successfully breed and thrive." For a moment, it is as though he silently accepts responsibility for all that has happened, but surprisingly, I don't hold any resentment towards him.

"Okay." I wait patiently for him to continue. Well, as patiently as someone can wait when you're standing next to a huge storm-creating machine.

"If the weather isn't suitable for the survival of the virus, then it is only a matter of time before the virus loses effect. Noah, I need you to go up there and switch it off."

He says it like it's easy.

"And you suggest I do that *how*?"

"I didn't make the machine, I'm not sure on how, exactly, the control panel works."

Neither am I.

He sighs, then continues, an exasperated breath of his final instruction. "I may be immune, Noah. But I do not possess such strength as you."

Although questioning this further seems like an idea that makes far more sense, I've never really been one for making sense. To my surprise, the door to the tower opens with more ease than I had thought it would. I guess the guys up there didn't really consider the idea of security when there is practically a hurricane on their doorway.

As soon as I am inside, I lose my act and become Noah again, running at an unbelievable pace up the winding staircase. My heart thumps faster than I think it ever has done. It continues to thump as the two workers in their plain, white suits catch sight of me, grab a hold of my shoulders. I manage to shake one off, but the other keeps a firm grip. He can't be much older than me, yet he is stronger. I had almost made it to the top floor—the floor I assume that contains the control panels for the manipulation of weather; the storm creating machine —but he pulls me to the floor below this, pushes me onto the ground in a small, dusty room, and locks the door, eyes warning me.

But there is more than just warning.

In his eyes are anger, sadness, and pain, all so intertwined that they may as well resemble that of the storm outside.

Liam

Riley paces back and forth by the side of the small fire we had lit to keep warm. We are not far from civilisation at all—the buildings are huge in their view—but still Riley is restless.

"Riley, you need to rest." She had exhausted herself from running Eastwards, desperation to find Noah filling her every bone.

"Liam, *please,*" her begging voice brings a flicker of memory to when we were so young, begging me to show her how to swim when she could barely walk.

She was so curious, so brave.

She still is.

"Not yet."

"Why not?"

"Because I'm your older brother, and you've gotta listen to me."

"You aren't that much older," she sighs with distress, before wandering off among some trees, looking around profoundly.

Riley

The branches move.

I turn to the others, gesturing for them to be quiet. Ebony drops Liam's guitar she had been holding to the floor, and the strings vibrate loudly against it. Liam covers his face with his hand, quickly looking at Ebony with slight disappointment, before holding his breath.

A young boy walks out from behind the branches. He looks a few years younger than Ebony, and he is wearing a plain white suit, but it is covered with dirt and snow. His eyes are not blank, but full of fear.

"It's okay, we won't hurt you," I whisper, raising my hands to indicate I am devoid of weapons. Instantly, his face lights up with trust, but the fear does not leave.

It is just no longer directed towards us.

"I can't fight for them. There must be another way we can protect ourselves." He begins to sob, tears running down his small, red cheeks.

"What is your name?" is all I can think to ask, so patiently I wait for an answer as the young boy appears to recollect his thoughts.

"Adam. Adam Williams," he pauses and looks at the floor. Why is that name so familiar? I read it somewhere, right? The missing…the immune.

"I've been on my own a while; I just want my m—"

"Adam?" a voice calls from the bushes, frail and nervous but still determined. She runs to him, to her son's voice, and embraces him. I watch for a while too long, enviously, and in that moment never have I wanted my mother's embrace more. It does not take long for me to acknowledge Liam and Ebony's faces are mirroring that of my own, a thousand memories of my mother and Ebony's mother flickering through their minds. It takes me a moment to swallow the lump in my throat before I look at Adam and his mother. She speaks before I can question her.

"You are immune too? Oh my God. Did you escape? I told my son to escape, but it took me forever to escape and then find him. I didn't know if he'd survive out here, not on his own. I prayed and prayed for him, I prayed all the time…he's alive…and, and…don't you see we can't fight? I can't KILL. That's what they want us to do, I'm sure of it. I'm sure…" Her words turn into sobs, incomprehensible. It reminds me of a book my father was reading underneath that I had begged him to show me. He was reading a section on Psychology, which stated how our strong feelings can result in our bodies not functioning how we intend them to, for instance, causing our words to become jumbled, causing tears even though we try to fight them back.

For a moment, I think back to how I feel around Noah. Vivid thoughts of how my heart beats faster than when I am running, or when a fluttering feeling rushes through my stomach, flood through my mind.

"Riley? Did you hear her? She is speaking to you," Liam says gently yet impatiently at the same time. He doesn't even wait for my answer before gesturing for the child's mother to speak for what I suppose is a repeat of whatever I have just missed.

"Are there others? Other immunes?"

"No—" Liam begins, but I cut him short. I take my rucksack off my shoulders, feel around desperately for the scraps of paper.

"If the missing are immune, then yes, there are," I say quickly. I can see Adam on the page, a little younger than he appears right now.

It takes only a half hour before Ebony has fixed the wounds of Adam and his mother, as well as helping them to build shelter as far out of sight as possible without us walking back where we had come.

"It's okay," Ebony says, kneeling down to the young boy. "We fight for 私たちの人々"

The young boy, Adam, repeats Ebony's words slowly, struggling to focus on anything other than her stare. I try to ignore his trance-like state when I gaze down at Ebony.

"What is '私たちの人々'?" I ask her, in between catching my breath which is quickly becoming shallow.

"Oh, yes, it is Japanese isn't it. My bad. It is …is how you say…our people. We fight for our people. We fight for the power to be completely ourselves, in all fullness All together." I smile at her, the small girl with the dark, brave eyes moving forward for what seems like an infinity, determination spreading through every inch of her weak bones.

We leave our camp for Adam and his mother before carrying on Eastwards. Ebony's words echo through my head for the entire journey, which seems longer than it is, because our speed has significantly slowed. When it finally slows to a standstill, we do not have time to appreciate the rest. Instead, we are all fixated towards the crowds of people, all dressed in white, all blank eyes, all gone. They hold weapons. Guns? None of us can form words, and I do not for one second expect us to.

"Right, okay, erm," Liam's thoughts are racing. I know because his eyebrows are creased, just like they always used to when he thought heavily as a child. "You guys listen to me. I'm serious, you listen to me, okay?"

We nod, handing our trust to him.

"Okay, good—" I can't hear anything else he is saying, not anymore. He pauses shortly after I stop listening, all of us focused solely on the voice of a man who seems to be speaking through a mouthpiece which echoes through the city upon some form of speaker system. As he talks, a thick layer of fog begins to submerge in the air. I run my fingers through it shakily, watching as it crawls up my arm.

"You are probably not aware, fellow soldiers, that some have become immune to the wondrous…gift that the government has given you."

He speaks, and I do not like his voice one bit. "The original medical scientist we have working for us seems somewhat opposed to the idea of creating a stronger virus to use on you all. So, I made one myself. It just needs… colder air, shall we say, hence all the smoke." Before his voice cuts out, I hear a malicious laughter escaping the mouthpiece.

Just like my father had done not long ago, Liam covers my nose and mouth with one hand, Ebony's with the other. We cooperate without saying a word; Our scarves become masks as we fight our way through the fog. Liam whispers through his own scarf. "If I remember right, that building over there," he begins to gesture with a shaking hand towards a building in a distance but catches his hand on a thorn from the bush that we are hiding behind.

"Liam, are you okay?" The bleed is pretty bad, and he winces. I expect Ebony to run over to him and help, but she doesn't.

"Its fine." And really, he means it. I watch as his wound heals before my eyes. Everything I have ever read about the human healing process goes against my own eyes, and I would be more astounded than I am if we didn't need to get out of here so quickly.

I am hallucinating, I have to be.

Then again, everything else I have seen over the last few days has been just as ethereal as this.

Liam catches me staring, whispers "Okay, Ri, sorry that I don't possess a crazy immunity-caused power as good as your own, you know, one that was worth protecting." I hear the hurt in his voice and go to comfort him, but he cuts me short, continuing what he had been saying previously.

"That building over there is where Dad works; me and Noah used to go there sometimes."

"His office in the Above?" I ask, thinking about underneath, but he nods.

"Yeah, in the city." I look where he is pointing, through masses of still, lifeless people, and see a white, tall office like building. Ebony and I follow him cautiously around a back path, not having to worry about leaving footprints behind because the pathways have seemingly been gritted down.

It surprises me for a moment that the door to the building opens almost effortlessly, but then I remember how everyone is not themselves and would not even try to get in unless they were ordered to.

Everyone, that is, apart from us.

The missing.

Inside, the bottom floor of the building is large and filled with what seems like hundreds of people dressed in white lab coats. We run behind a white wall, shielding ourselves from the people dressed in white, shielding ourselves from this huge, white abyss.

We are all glancing down at our own appearances; faces covered with dirt, hair—wet and matted—still blanketed with snowflakes, our clothing a mixture of too big and too small and everything in between. To our left, there is a room with the door a crack open. Liam puts his ear to it for a second—listening for others—and then pushes me and Ebony in silently.

"There's gotta be…" he starts, but his eyes light up quickly after as he looks behind a desk and sees a coat hanger with several white lab coats hanging from it. He grabs three for each of us. Just as he is doing it, he catches sight of a young man, no older than twenty, holding a communication device.

"Erm, sir—" he begins, but he is cut short as Liam walks up to him.

"I wouldn't if I were you," he confronts the young man's nametag. "Charles. I used to see you when I was stuck here, imprisoned as one of their soldiers. I heard you complaining about the world now. We are trying to fix it. So, if you wanna cling on to any amount of hope that the world will be good again, then you need to trust us and not say a word about what we are doing right now. Do you hear me?"

A long pause.

"What is it? I'm kind of in the middle of something here," comes a voice from his communication device. I'm pretty sure it's the same voice that just announced the newer, stronger virus release.

"Nothing, sir," he says with finality, switching off the device and handing it to Liam. Liam takes it and tucks it firmly into his lab coat pocket before asking the young man, "Do you know where Dr Carter's office is?"

"Yeah, it's out this door, and then five doors to your left. Stand up straight, don't look at anybody, and if anyone asks what you are doing just say that you have an urgent request from the council and don't have time to talk." He pauses for a second and looks at Ebony, whose lab coat is dragging across the floor. "And maybe take the lab coat off her. She's too young. You're better just saying that you're taking her for a stronger injection or something."

Liam nods once.

As we walk out, I am wondering what exactly we are going to do to help. There is no plan that any of us have come up with—not aloud at least—and it feels as though we are walking aimlessly through this mass of workers for the new world. Still, I know we have one goal in mind, and that for me is a goal I cannot stop panicking over.

"You think Noah will be with Dad?"

"I hope Noah will be with Dad. I'm clinging to that hope."

I decide I am too.

It's not long before we reach the office, but there is no one in there and I am filled all at once with dread.

"Where *are* they?" I want to cry, let the room fill with my tears, but I don't.

Ebony grabs my hand and whispers, "It is okay. We will find them." For her, I wipe my tears away and try to think again, which is hard when there are too many thoughts pacing through your mind, and you cannot focus on just the necessary ones.

"You looking for Doctor Carter?"

Another man, older but still dressed in white, gestures towards Ebony and says, "I can take her to him if you want."

"NO!" I scream, feeling the ground begin to shake beneath me. The power is too much, and it feeds on my fear and need to protect Ebony. The man struggles to make sense of our surroundings, and alarm reaches his own face as he realises the threat. He grasps Ebony's small shoulders, hard, and pulls her away from us, fingernails digging into her delicate skin.

"Please, let her go!" I howl, the words catching painfully in my throat. The ground continues to shake, a whirlwind of emotion.

In my peripheral vision, I can regard Liam's grey eyes, flitting between Ebony and I.

"Riley, breathe," he orders. I turn towards him, the storm I am creating blowing through my hair, and watch as he gestures back towards Ebony.

Ebony's dark eyes are wide, celestial almost. And they are fixated on the man who has left deep, red marks on Ebony's neck with his firm grip.

He is hurting her.

But before I can attempt to walk towards them, Ebony begins to speak, focusing intently upon his own gaze.

"You will let us go. あなたは私たちを手放します," she speaks softly, an unearthly resonance leaving her voice and leading the man into a trance. Instantly, he drops Ebony to the floor, and she gasps for breath. Rapidly, we pace out of the door and outside, back where we had been, among the crowds. The fog is still there, and we breathe, forgetting for a second, but nothing happens.

Our immunity must be untouchable.

"Come on," Liam holds on to Ebony's shoulders and gently pushes her through the crowd, while I stand on the other side of her protectively, gaze wondering from person to person. Out here it is mostly the gone; their eyes are clouded and white, almost so white that you cannot see their pupils. Their expressions are non-existent; instead, they just stare without really staring. We walk through them staring straight ahead, silently praying they do not realise we aren't working for the government. I notice how Liam keeps his head down, afraid in case another worker recognises him from his time here. In an instant I feel this never-ending sadness throughout my entire body as I imagine him here, trying to work out why God let this became our world.

It's quick that these thoughts, the sadness, is replaced by sudden panic as we are all grasped by a man, and I recognise him because I recognise his potent, dominant voice.

"I think you all better come with me."

Chapter Thirteen

Liam

I can see them, and I refuse to take my eyes off them. Riley has her head in her knees, long hair covering her body as she inhales and exhales deeply. Ebony's small hands grip the prison-like bars that surround her. I can tell she is trying to mask the fear which courses through her veins, but doesn't quite make it to her face. Although I can see them, I can't reach them. We are all divided from one another in prison-like cells. Straight ahead of us is Thomas, the leader of this ill-disposed government, walking back and forth and muttering, "What am I going to do with you?"

"Let them go, preferably," I murmur, locking eyes with him.

"You're just like your father; he has become so disobedient recently. It's most disconcerting."

"Disobedience is not a bad thing when what you are obeying is wrong."

"You know what?" Thomas makes sure he is staring practically into my soul, but I'm not fazed by it. In fact, I've always wanted to stare him down, to challenge him.

The main soul behind this deranged world that Riley calls the Above. "I'll show you what you should be obeying."

"If you think you're gonna successfully brainwash us or something, then I'd give up now, *sir,*" I say the last part through gritted teeth, mocking his role of authority. He doesn't answer, instead he walks out, searching for something.

I look at Ebony and Riley. Ebony has tears in her eyes and Riley is trying to reassure her. At first, I think she's scared, but instead, she says, "I want to help them, Riley. We can't do anything in here."

Thomas is back in a second, holding a disk. I haven't seen one of them in years, so I don't expect Riley to even know what it is but it's clear she does when she mouths, "What is he gonna show us?" I just shake my head and watch, completely unknowing.

"When you watch this, you'll change your mind," he says it with finality, but I don't listen. We watch as he inserts the disk into an old DVD player. The screen flickers a bit before it turns on, displaying what seems like an old news report.

The screen projects a blood-curdling war; fleeting images of weaponised cities and screaming people seeking refuge. Brutality and deaths, an encompassment of gore to which Ebony and Riley flinch.

I knew the war before the storm had been bad. But I didn't realise just quite how bad.

A news reporter stands in front of the massacre in protective clothing, talking hurriedly. "Yes, the war is spreading, expansive and relentless—" But before he can continue, he is shot.

Another life amounting to nothing.

"These people," Thomas begins, smug as he sees our horrified faces. "These innocent people died for nothing. Only, how could we live? We weren't fighting. There were too many people like that man on the screen there, reluctant to use violence for humanity. But is that not the only way to stop them?" He pauses, waiting for a response. I just stare him dead in the eye, while he changes the disk to another. Ebony and Riley turn away this time, but they are alert, listening, bracing themselves for whatever is to come.

"Yet another bombing today in London," speaks a news reporter. "Officials are calling for a fight back, but many members of the public appear to be in disagreement with this plan of action because of various beliefs. It seems even a conscription would not force these people to neglect their beliefs and agree to use violence in a war."

I remember these attacks, dad's face as he was on important phone calls constantly, Riley wanting to go outside and play but our father being worried for our safety.

"You know," Riley begins to speak, a new bravery surfacing from within her. "There are other ways to fight. Control is not one of them. Once you begin to control, you take away the knowledge of what people are fighting for. You take away their light, their life. YOU become the enemy in the war."

Thomas grimaces. "Control is the only way to stop evil."

Riley says, "Control is evil." She walks to the bars, the ones separating us, and grabs a hold of them, resting her face against them so she can maintain eye contact with Thomas.

"I admire your bravery," says Thomas, and to my surprise he lets us out one by one so we are standing together. I want to believe maybe he has an inch of faith in us, in what we are saying. Enough to let us go completely. But he is holding the key to the main door, walking towards it, laughing. "Unfortunately, bravery for what you *believe* is not permitted in this scenario."

From seemingly out of nowhere, Thomas pulls three chairs across the floor and aligns them precisely. He then forces us down, one by one, assigning us each a chair.

Ebony begins to say "You will…" in Japanese, but Thomas refuses to look her in the eye.

"You don't think I have any idea of your little weird traits? I won't fall into that trap, I am afraid." The door locks behind him, and we are left standing in this room, neither of us speaking a word until we are certain he is no longer within earshot.

The room is dark, lit only with dim, grey lights. One chair sits facing our direction, and I don't have to be exceedingly smart to understand what is about to happen.

Thomas appears in the room, an ugly grimace upon his face. There is no sound coming from the room, but we hear a parade of footsteps advancing towards us from outside our door.

Thomas's sinister smile expands as multiple people in lab coats and protective gear pace through the door, carrying a mass of equipment.

When I look closer, I can see electrodes… used for brain scanning.

This has happened to me before. To Noah and I.

Only, the experimenter was my father.

Riley

Until this moment, I had forgotten being in my home underneath at such a young age, with my father and mother reassuring me that the electrodes on my scalp were not going to harm me. They had tightly clasped on my skull, like they are now, gripping, all-encompassing.

My father had made notes, observing my behaviour, the scans on his computer screen. He had fallen back in shock when the ground shook, but I assumed it had been the storm in the Above.

I never understood what he had been doing until now.

"You are… so special. You might be just what this world needs," he had whispered.

"There are others like her? You said?" said my mother.

"Not this strong. She has to be protected until she knows how to use her powers."

"How long—"

"Fifteen years, Emelia. She will leave, we all will, when she turns eighteen."

I hold the memory in my mind as though I will lose it again, but I am back in the moment, wincing at the cold metal numbing my scalp.

I turn my face slightly to look at Liam, only to find he is staring right back at me. I want him to be brave, but in his eyes all I can make out is indescribable amount of fear.

My heart beats, fast.

My chair clatters, just a little.

Thomas raises his head and nods slowly, and I stare at him wide-eyed, fastened hands shaking from behind my back.

Ebony begins to cry "YOU WILL STOP—" but she is cut short.

"It's not your turn, yet," one of the people says, with slits for eyes and fists clenched. He tapes Ebony's mouth so she cannot speak, only hum desperately against the material.

"Tough guy first." He gestures to Liam.

Liam shakes his chair, tries to move across to the door, but it won't budge.

I have never seen him this scared.

My stomach sinks.

One of the people – a man no older than twenty, eyes almost as numb as those upon the gone – clutches a gun in his hand. No words can escape my mouth before he shoots Liam in the foot, pain flooding across his face. He winces for a moment, but in the blink of an eye, I watch as his wound heals. It turns to nothing but a faded scar, barely resembling any form of conflict.

I turn to the screen we had watched the war upon, now holding the scans of Liam's brain. His own scan is next to a printed image of a brain scan labelled 'the gone', which appears to be dull, lifeless, apart from one section lit up only slightly.

In comparison, Liam's brain is glowing. Like a mass of embers from a dying fire.

It's astonishing.

"The young girl, now," they say in unison, appearing to obey an order from Thomas which I myself cannot hear.

The tape is ripped from her mouth, while one of the individuals surrounding her puts himself forward, looks straight into her eyes.

"あなたは私を放っておきます！You WILL leave me ALONE!" She screams, her eyes darker than ever, glowing yet colourless, all at once.

Instantaneously, the man falls backwards, crawls away from Ebony.

Her brain scan is now upon the screen, another flurry of ablaze embers.

The tape is forced back upon her mouth before she can so much as whisper another word.

"Riley Carter."

I take a deep breath, feel the beads of sweat dripping down my forehead, threatening to land in my eyes and make me flinch.

Thomas watches from the window, challenging me almost. He nods.

And then I am screaming.

Pain pounds through my head, making my blood boil. The pain pulsates towards the back of my spine, and I jolt back, as though in response to a stab wound.

"STOP!" I cry, wincing through the trauma. In my mind, images of Noah, my parents, my brother, and Ebony, spiral until I am overcome with unfaltering despondency.

And then I feel it, exactly what they wanted to see. The world around me begins to spin; an incoming tsunami consumes me from within.

I stand, my hands breaking free simultaneously.

There is a crack in the window, and Thomas stares straight at it as it grows, evolves into a gaping obstruction. I watch, tears falling from my eyes, as the glass shatters, and Thomas orders them to stop.

I fall to the floor and am about to rest my head to the ground, weakness overcoming me.

But then I see the screen, my scan.

"That's the thing with this virus," breathes Thomas, as I stare evermore at the screen, fixated. "We did not anticipate for such non-malleable, powerful brains such as your own. Especially not yours, Riley Carter."

It is not just glowing with embers.

It is ablaze with an indestructible fire.

"It is clear the stronger mutation of the virus within the air did not impact your immune bodies in the slightest. James!" He calls.

My father walks in and I want to scream. I want to scream even more when I see what my father is holding; three needles, filled with oozing fluid. His expression is sorry, his eyes are red and hurt, and I can see how much he wants to run over to us and embrace us, but he won't. He won't but there's a reason he won't; he has a plan because I can see it there in his eyes.

Liam can't.

He breaks free from his chair and runs over to my father before I can reach out to stop him, shouting and shouting and shouting. His hands are cuffed into fists, but he doesn't want to hit my father, he is just angry and scared all at once.

My father grabs Liam's shoulder and injects him.

"No…" I don't even think the word leaves my mouth, because it is soon after that Ebony's shoulder is injected with the fluid, and then within seconds my father has my shoulder. His grip is gentle, reassuring. I'm not sure if I am imaging it or not, but I am almost certain he whispers quickly in my ear, "If this changes you, it won't last long in the new weather conditions. I promise."

Then I feel it, the fluid invading my cells, coursing its way through the absoluteness of my body. I want to speak but I can't.

"This is an even stronger version of the virus, version 3.0. If this doesn't make you see the way I want you to see, nothing else will." Thomas laughs maliciously, and I begin to wonder if the real reason he did all this was power, but then I stop wondering and fall to the ground because the world is spinning and my head is pounding. But while everything hurts, while I can feel *something* changing my body, it is not changing *me*. I feel stronger than ever, as though my body has welcomed this fluid and used it to its own advantage.

I look over at Liam. His shoulder does not look as though anything has even touched it. Any bruises or minor injuries he had before are gone; not just scars, but gone completely. His gaze is still the same; he is just watching me worriedly. I look at Ebony now, and she seems fine too. But it is as though the bravery that drives her loyalty has increased because I can see it in her eyes, the way she stands and looks at Thomas, the way she says, "We're stronger than you think. We are gonna save our people."

It's as though her immune system—no, her spirit—has fought back with more voice than before.

I feel a bittersweet burst of happiness course through my veins.

And now I am looking at my hands.

They are…no, they aren't.

They're glowing, an orange hue that brings light to the dark room, and I don't know what's happening, my emotion now depicting hope as though it is a canvas.

"You WILL let us leave! あなたは私たちを去らせます," Ebony cries, looking round until every person in the room, including Thomas, is in a trance-like state. Everyone, apart from my father.

They make a pathway free so that we can walk towards the door, but I am the last to leave, locking eyes with my father.

"You knew this would make us even stronger, didn't you? Have the opposite effect it would have had on the gone," I ask.

"I had a pretty good idea. I know what you are capable of, Riley, you and your brother. Ebony could only have been the same. If the virus initially had such a profound, unexpected effect on you, a stronger version – even stronger than the second – would only enhance such effect."

I gulp. "So, you really are on our side?"

"Yes, Riley. I really am."

Before I know it, tears begin to flood my face, and my throat croaks. "I'm so sorry I didn't believe you." I cry.

Simultaneously, my skin becomes ablaze with bright colour and light; an optic depiction of my emotions, a mind dissociated from the mechanical regime of the government.

"I'm sorry—" I repeat. I try to wipe my tears away, to seem brave. But my father stops me, puts his hand upon my shoulder.

"The bravest thing you will ever do, Riley, is to show your tears. Don't hide your emotion – you are more special than you will ever know."

I want to smile, but I can't help but notice Liam in the doorway, sadness in his eyes.

The possibility still in the back of his mind that my father doesn't see us as his children, but simply as soldiers.

And Liam was not the protected soldier, the main piece of the puzzle to end this war.

He still believes he was incapable, insignificant.

Not worth protecting.

I try to plead with him through my eyes, show him this is the furthest thing from truth, but he looks away.

"Come on," he breathes, looking to the ground. "We gotta go."

Chapter Fourteen

"In here," Liam orders, and my father, Ebony and I follow.

So far, we have made it past four guards patrolling the surrounding area, using both Ebony's and my strengths.

"At least I'm wound-resistant," Liam had murmured to himself each time. His grey eyes sad, but focused.

The room we enter is misty and dark, accompanied by an unpleasant damp smell. A closet room, consisting of a multitude of white lab coats and white uniforms. Clothes deducting each individual in the camps to a singular entity.

We huddle together tightly, awaiting my father's words.

"Firstly," he whispers, looking at both Liam and I. "I would like to say your mother is safe. Ri, it was part of our plan for her and I to leave before you. Of course, I wasn't aware you were going to pretend to be dead to remain safe—"

Liam interrupts hastily. "I'm sorry? Acting skills as well, huh? What can't you do, Riley?"

Ebony stifles back a giggle, before my father continues.

"And Noah?" I ask. His name is hard to say aloud, but I do it anyway. "Do you know where he is?"

"He's already helping us, actually. The weather that fuels this virus, it's artificial, much like its viral counterpart. Once the cold is disabled, the virus will be too. Noah is making his way to the control panel as we speak."

I breathe an exasperated breath.

"He'll need back up."

"I'll go," I almost shout the words, longing to assure myself he is safe.

My father nods once.

"Liam, you and Ebony will need to disguise yourself among the gone. When they begin to wake from the virus' manipulation, they will need the first people they see to be those who they can trust; those who know the truth about what has happened to them. Riley, to get to Noah, you'll have to walk among them too."

Liam looks at my father with utter bewilderment. "We can't send Riley and Ebony out there. One wrong move and they could be killed."

"Liam, not only are you forgetting Ebony was born in these camps, but you are forgetting that both Riley and Ebony have strengths hard to comprehend."

Liam winces at the words. "And me? What good am I out there, exactly?"

I silently plead with my father to reassure Liam that he is significant, that his own immune body is powerful and needed beyond belief.

"Your body is practically bullet proof, son. You yourself will simply not have to worry about getting hurt."

That's it. That's all he says. Not he has the strength to help others, but that he himself will be protected.

Ebony can see the hurt in Liam's eyes as much as I can.

When my father isn't looking, I try to rest my hands upon Liam's shoulder, but he shrugs me away.

"Focus on the task at hand, Riley. Focus on helping Noah, on saving the gone. This world isn't going to be safe again, not without you."

It's not long before I am among the gone, their faces as still as a thousand portraits.

I want to look around at them all but I can't, so I just look straight ahead like I have been for the past who knows how long, willing this moment to end. In the far distance, I can see Thomas and the crew who had placed electrodes upon our scalps, searching the crowd desperately. For a moment, Thomas's eyes investigate a crowd of the gone which stand scarily close to me. But soon enough he is gone, focus diverted towards something else. Despite this, his malevolent gaze lingers in my mind; it is almost impossible to erase it, stubborn almost as much as the virus.

Everyone is in white uniform, blank eyes staring straight ahead. I am still wearing the white lab coat from earlier, which blends me in enough.

Small step by small step, I diverge away from Liam, Ebony, and my father. All I have to find Noah is my father's brief description of the weather tower, and doubt floods me as I slowly walk upon the snow-washed cement of the ground.

I try not to collide with the gone but it is near impossible; they are everywhere, like a swarm of flies with no clear purpose. In my peripheral vision I can see a group of them with guns, shooting at wooden targets in the shape of people. The targets read 'THE ATTACKERS', but watching them shoot solemnly, it is hard to know who exactly the attackers are.

The reason for why this war continues.

Suddenly, I feel entangled by this government, by this so-called civilisation. I want to erase the numbers tattooed upon Liam, Noah and Ebony, clean from their skin.

I feel anger and despair and fear, all at once.

My skin is not glowing, no longer an outward depiction of my previous euphoria.

Instead, the ground cement beneath me begins to crack, and I feel as though I am surfing the onset of an earthquake.

Breathe, Riley. I try to calm myself, but it is near impossible. With every tremble my body produces, the ground produces more, and I double over in pain. I long for the embrace of Noah, think about how his touch had calmed me immediately, how the emotional fire within me had felt extinguished by an abounding river…

His grasp heals emotional pain. That's his strength. I know when to bring the storm, and he knows when to bring the calm.

Upon my hot, enraged skin, I can feel the necklace he had given me, fastened loosely around my neck. It is cold, comforting. And though the claim surrounding the St. Christopher – that it keeps you safe – may be an old wives' tale, it is a piece of Noah.

A piece of calm.

I breathe. The grounds shaking slows to near standstill.

I can feel a dozen eyes upon me, and I know in this moment, I cannot afford to be fearful.

I push myself up from the ground, slowly looking around me to assess my bearings.

But I know there is only one way I can find him quick enough.

My heart races as I walk up to two authority figures, distinguished by their lab coats.

"Noah Jordan has been captured. I have been ordered to go and help ordain the situation," I say this in the most monotone-like voice I can manifest, making sure not to look them directly in the eyes.

"Noah Jordan?" They say his name as a question. This is good, sort of, because it means they shouldn't know who I am, or that I am immune.

At least, I hope.

It's a huge risk, but without the courage I won't make any progress.

"Noah Jordan," I confirm, knowing they'll have some way of finding him. I erase all that I feel for Noah in my voice, and I don't like the way I say his name when I do. Because I speak his name in grey, but in my heart his name is a thousand colours.

"Have you been shown a photo of this man? Are you familiar with his appearance?"

"Yes." I know his face almost like I know the palm of my hand. Completely and not at all, both at once.

One of them takes out a camera device from their jacket pocket and shows me images of a series of rooms which I assume are all within this small section, this camp, in London. Instantly, my eyes are drawn to my father, Liam and Ebony, walking separately among the gone. Liam stands close behind Ebony, but this doesn't stop her bottom lip from quivering, her knees from shaking. I gulp, drawing my eyes away from them and scanning the other rooms for Noah.

Then I see him, and everything inside of me hurts. He is trying to pull away from a guard who has him grasped tightly by his wrist, so much so that ugly red indents are left upon it.

I want to scream.

But instead, I nod once, point at Noah and say, "Directions to this room."

"That's…the weather tower. Are you sure you were asked to—"

"Yes," I interrupt, a little impatiently, most probably a mistake.

"It's about a mile straight ahead," one of them says. The other looks at him, alarmed.

"We better check this…"

I begin walking.

The other man gets out a communication device. "Erm, Sir…"

Thomas answers.

"We got a girl, around eighteen, 5-foot, brown hair, headed towards the weather tower. You requested that, right sir?"

Thomas starts shouting inaudibly.

They call out to me.

I am running.

To my bewilderment, I begin to laugh, and my skin starts to glow again, everything in me a golden light which radiates and guides my way.

A mile straight ahead.

Chapter Fifteen

Noah

These people are seriously prepared for anything. They have prison bars up here, and it appears as though I am prisoner. It's like they knew an immune-with-an-actual-soul would invade their tower.

I sit against the wall of this small, barred section, watching the guard who brought me here pace back and forth. He only looks a couple years older than me, maybe twenty-two like Liam, with slick blond hair and headphones in his ears which remind me of the night before they found me.

It feels like forever since I made that playlist for Riley. I don't know if she ever got to hear it. Crap, I don't know where she is now. Music is one of the phenomenon's that express everything there is to express about life, and she deserved to hear its beauty.

And then I went and got found.

"Hey," I try and get the man's attention. At this point, there really isn't much more I can lose, and he doesn't appear threatening. Instead, he looks kinda sad, and I feel a little sympathetic towards him. He looks over and raises an eyebrow, slowly taking out one headphone from his ear.

"I...shouldn't be talking to you."

I laugh. I really can't help myself, because I can see in his eyes how much he *wants* to talk to me. They are filled to the brim with pure curiosity, and I wonder how long it has been since he had human interaction with someone who was not gone or a member of this reckless government.

"Ah, like you shouldn't really be listening to music because its message might distract you from your purpose in the war, right?"

He looks almost threatened, so I smile.

"Hey, mate, I'm messing with you." I hold my hands up from behind the bars; a symbol of acquaintance. "I won't tell anyone. It's not like I can anyway. What're you listening to?"

"Erm, it's nothing. Just a tune my old man used to like." But he shows me anyway, reaching out what I think is an old mobile phone. It displays a picture of the album, along with the song title and music artist. I raise an eyebrow and question, "Freedom? By George Michael?"

"Yeah."

He looks panicked, overwhelmed. I see a thousand and one thoughts spiralling through his mind, consuming him like a storm.

And then I envision calm.

"Don't you think these people deserve freedom to keep their beliefs? Don't you think they shouldn't be forced into using violence to fight?" I look him in the eyes when I ask it, reach out through the bars to touch his shoulder and wait as for what I always see from my physical contact. Almost immediately I see it; the mitigation of his spiralling emotions.

But what he does next astonishes me. I stand in bewilderment as he walks over to the bars and unlocks the door keeping me behind them. As he does it, he asks, "What exactly did you have in plan?"

I smile.

"Welcome aboard the let's-take-back-faith-for-humanity train," he laughs, moving his arms in the motion of a train passing through the streets of London. "If I'm honest, I had a half-plan. The half part was to stop this weather. I just have absolutely no idea on earth how to go about that process."

"You're lucky you are with someone who can bring the other half to your plan and actually carry it out successfully."

"You know how to work that thing?"

"That's my job. Come on."

We trek up the winding stairs, an odyssey I really don't have the energy for. But it's not long before we reach the controls room, and as I peer out the window above the controls panel, I can see the cold air pumping out of the building. It rises into the sky and fills everything around us. This room is even colder than the one we were in below, and I didn't think that'd be possible. In fact, it seemed beyond the bounds of possibility that anywhere could be colder than down there.

I stand corrected.

The guard is practically attacking the control panel; it looks like he has been wanting to put an end to this weather for a really, really long time.

There is nothing else to do but stare either at him engaging in something that confuses me too much to try and help, or to carry on looking out the window, and so I decide to do the latter. But then she is there and time stops because there are people running after her and I have no idea what to do. Everything in me feels like it is going to explode. And it's not just because I am seeing her running from guards with guns, but it is because she is glowing. Literally glowing, light radiating from her skin.

"Hey, a little help over here?" It takes me a while to pull my eyes off of her, but I do. He is pulling a lever which seems as though it hasn't been moved for years, and it probably hasn't if it has been maintaining the cold. I help him pull it, and then it is done and for a moment nothing changes.

But then the sound of an engine or something that I hadn't even realised was present stops, and so does the cold air which had been pulsating out of the building. The wind outside is gradually slowing to a standstill, and even though we are not outside it is clear that the atmosphere is beginning to become serene.

"How long do you think it'll be before the virus begins to die off?"

"The weather will still be minus degrees for a good two hour minimum, and even then, the virus will only gradually begin to subside. Who knows how badly the damage has been done already."

"A lot, we know that. What we don't yet know is whether or not we can reverse it. But let's pray to God that he's gonna fill those cold souls with love again." I place my hand on his shoulder for a second as a gesture of thanks, and a last dose of calm, before pacing down the winding stairs faster than I think my body is capable of.

One thing I am uncertain of is how much time we have before we reach each other, and I hope more than anything we do.

Liam

I can't see her face, but just her black, plaited hair which falls messily behind her shoulders, and her toy poking out of her pocket. But I don't have to be able to see her face to know she is trembling.

Sometimes, the bravest people we know can be the ones who feel the most fear.

My eyes are fixated upon Ebony, protecting her even though she is more capable at protecting herself than I am her.

But then I spot my father, the shock on his face starkly contrasting to the paper-white of his skin. He raises his head, closes his grey eyes, and seemingly waits for another small, drop of snow.

Nothing.

Instead, we are merely welcomed by a light breeze, nowhere near as sharp as had recollected it to be.

He did it. Noah did it. He must have done.

"Do you feel that?" I hear Thomas's shout abhorrent shout from the near distance. I am taller than most of the crowd, so it is not long before I see him among the thousands of heads.

"What?" Someone shouts back to him.

"The weather…something isn't right." Inevitably, he looks up towards the weather tower and so do I. There is no longer a visible bitter, cold fog drumming out of it. Instead, it just looks like there is merely remnants of what had been.

"Maybe something is faulty," the other voice calls out.

"Faulty?" Thomas mocks him, annoyance building more than I thought was possible on his face. I narrow my eyes at him across the crowd, squinting to watch his every move. Ebony and my father do the same. "There's not been a single fault on that thing in the fifteen years it has been running. My guys are always monitoring it." He starts to pace back and forth, the first sign of panic I have seen from him sweeping across his face.

"You want me to go up there and have a look?" The other voice asks, a desperate attempt to console Thomas. He is hesitant, but he realises he doesn't have much of a choice.

"Yes," he responds, before walking through the array of people expeditiously.

Riley

I don't stop because I can hear more steps and from the panic I hear in them, from the breathing that occupies them, I know they're Noah's. And when I think of him even more light floods through me, which I am grateful for because maybe he can see where I am a little better, which would make things a whole lot easier considering my vision right now is extremely blurred. I don't know if

107

that is due to weakness, or the tears that are flowing like a waterfall out of my eyes. But either way, it doesn't help my journey.

I want to turn around and see how far the guards are behind me, but if I do I know it might make me even a fraction slower. Instead, I feel for the St. Christopher around my neck, which also makes me a fraction slower. But I don't care because it is my calm and I won't let them take that away from me. They took away everything that made everyone hear a human, a soul, and I refuse to let them take it from the rest of the people I love. I won't ever let them do it again.

He's running out the door, his hair flying in the wind, his breath fast and painful, beads of sweat rolling down his forehead. When I see him looking at me, I know he doesn't even care right now about the light shining from me, he isn't questioning it, he is questioning my safety, and I feel a burst of love from him as he carries on pacing towards me. But then he stops, and behind him there is a young guard.

"I'm so sorry," he says to Noah. "Mate, I'm so sorry, they're watching me." And he injects him with the viral fluid: Virus 3.0. I wait apprehensively as Noah feels the liquid soar through his body, and I cannot help but fear the worst, despite knowing he is going to be more than okay. I can see in his eyes right through to his spirit, and now, without even feeling his touch, tranquillity soars over me. When he recovers from the initial shock, he lightly pushes the guard away and I watch as the guard seems bewildered but relieved all at once.

They grasp my arms from behind but I dare let them grab my courage. I let courage bloom like a lotus, rising from beneath the mud to above the clouds, out of the darkness and into the light. With that, I can see everything in my body as a pulsating glimmer of energy to which even Noah needs to look away. It blinds the guards and then I run again, and I reach him and slow my breath, counting to ten and then back again, and as I do so the light fades and then I am in his arms and he is in mine and I am never, never, never going to let go.

The gone

Everything is dark. Sometimes, we think thoughts of family are coming but they never do, and all we feel is numbness. We don't care because there is something in us and it has taken everything away, dulled our senses. We cannot think for ourselves so, while in our abyss, we think for those in charge because if they tell us what to do it is easier. We trust in them and we have trusted in them since we can remember; it takes too much energy to try and challenge our thoughts. Words of submission are our familiarity, and everything else is foreign. If we hear anything foreign, we are taught to erase it because it'll just make our job harder.

The air doesn't quite feel the same today. The unfamiliarity is messing with our minds, but we can't help but feel that part of us wants to welcome it.

We try to focus. Good, everyone is holding their weapons. This is what we were meant to do, to protect ourselves, to fight. Training is the same as always.

But the air…

There is light soaring past, and it feels like something somewhere in us has been switched back on. Even though it hurts, we want to reach out to the light, but it takes too much energy so we just stare straight ahead and do nothing.

Is that… emotion? A tear?

It is wiped away.

Then we pick up our weapons and carry-on training.

Chapter Sixteen

Riley

Noah pulls back from me and suddenly his body is stiff, absorbed by something behind me. But his stiffness doesn't appear to be as a result of feeling threatened. Instead, he just seems fully captivated by thought. I reluctantly pull back from him too, following his gaze behind me. The guard who had been chasing me must've lost sight a while back, because he seems to have been replaced by a familiar face.

The old woman.

Everything is happening in too little time and I am starting to feel overwhelmed, the whole world spinning, the ground shaking.

Noah touches my arm, and I am instantly entangled in a calm trance.

"Why are you here? It's too dangerous." Her grey hair appears more vibrant than it was when I last saw her, her eyes blue gems nested upon her face. She smiles once and then again, each smile better than the first.

"Who is this?" Noah asks me, while looking, captivated, at the woman.

"One of the missing, the immune. One of us." I beam. Though I am fearful for her safety, it is reassuring to have someone else here who has a mind of their own.

In answer to my question, the old woman responds, "Did you really think I'd let you fight this battle alone?" Her smirk is contagious. She continues softly, "I had to make sure you were okay."

I return to full seriousness, put my palm upon her shoulder and remind her of the danger we are in. One more of us means one more threat to Thomas, but it also means one more target he will send his army to kill.

The woman appears to read my thoughts when she says, "There will be even less of an army in under two hours."

"Under two hours?" echo promptly.

Noah's green eyes lock mine when he utters "Two hours until the virus starts to lose its effect."

Excitement surges through my body for an instant, but this is quickly replaced by panic.

"If the virus loses effect on the gone, then what will happen to us?"

How can we fight the government when we are powerless?

The old woman grins smugly, while reaching into her coat pocket. She takes out a crumbled piece of paper, filled with type-written notes.

I almost instantly recognise the notes from when we were being experimented upon.

"Look here," she whispers. Her finger points to the words *'unanticipated virus effect on immunes will NOT diminish in any circumstance – permanent alteration to the minds of these individuals.'*

"How did you get a hold of this?" Noah asks, astounded.

The woman shrugs, declares "I have my ways," and I stifle back laughter.

And that's when I feel it.

The conversation begins to blur, and my head is spinning. Suddenly, I am overcome by exhaustion, the strong effects of the virus upon my body finally engaging an unbearable amount of fatigue.

I sway a little, and Noah quickly grabs my shoulders with a certain gracefulness I do not think I could exhibit, supporting my weight with his own.

"Hey," the young guard calls from inside, an apologetic tone. He shows what looks like had been a camera, now smashed. "I've broken the cameras so they can't see inside the tower. I don't know how long we got but you better come in here now—she don't look too good." He gestures towards me. It feels as though I am fading in and out of consciousness as Noah half carries me inside, the old woman also holding me for support. I can feel the compassion and calm radiating from him, not just figuratively but literally; it is warm and bright and it makes my skin tingle.

His love is selfless.

It is a while before I begin to feel better. The young guard gave us some water before he left to keep watch outside.

I am leaning against the wall and Noah is looking at me in the same concerned way he looked at me when we first met. It gives me goose bumps, but the kind that don't feel bad at all.

"Why are all these people being kept in the darkness?" Noah suddenly asks to no one in particular, not really expecting an answer.

But his grandmother answers, "Diversity is light, but embracing this can and has caused disagreement and violence, so it can hurt. "Remember those early days after you first saw the light? Those were the hard times, targets of every kind of abuse." She is silent for a minute. Then she says, "We'll stay with it and survive, trusting all the way." I recognise those words. My mother told them to me when I was little, every night before I went to sleep. I used to tell her maybe it'd be easier if I didn't feel anything; not scared or imprisoned or angry. But she told me to keep every ounce of emotion and light that I had, even if sometimes it hurt. So, I think I know what the old woman means. We'll stay with our thoughts and emotions like the gone should have been able to. We will trust it, even if it hurts us.

That's when Noah says, "Thomas didn't stay with it, did he? He took it all away from them to stop the attacks, when really he is just as bad as the attackers." He says this as a fact, not as a question. No one answers, because there is no need to. All the pieces of the puzzle seem to fit now, and it is hurting my mind because it all makes too much sense and I hate that it is undeniably true. An artificial virus was released that only breeds in cold weather—my father helped create it—and it takes away everything that makes humanity, well, humanity. Emotion overwhelms me and the light starts up again. For the first time, I allow myself to be fully enchanted by it, wondering how on earth a stronger version of the virus could make this happen.

"How long do we have?"

"Just over an hour," Noah reassures me, putting his hand on my shoulder after passing me a hot mug of water. But I almost drop it as the door handle begins to jolt.

We hold our breath, but it is my father who rushes in, Dr James Carter, closing the door hurriedly behind him.

I sit up quickly, ignoring the pounding in my head. Noah pulls me closer, but I dare look away from my father.

"Liam? Ebony?"

"Still on the main grounds," he asserts while catching his breath. He then proceeds between gasps of exhaustion. "As soon as the gone wake from this trance, it's us against the government. Expansive confusion is going to be a critical side effect. We'll need them to console the gone, but we need you to fight back against whatever combat the government is planning."

"She's exhausted," Noah argues, his voice hoarser than my own. "How do you expect only her to fight? Aren't we NOT supposed to be playing pieces in their game?"

"Noah," my father begins. "You are not playing pieces, but it is only you who can end the game."

For a moment, I had forgotten the woman hunched over in the corner opposite to Noah and I, but she stands, making her presence known.

"We have more than just Riley and Noah." She reaches, for a second time, into her pocket. Another smirk embellishes itself upon her face as she brings out a camera device identical to those of the council's.

All exhaustion I had felt just moments ago is eradicated immediately, replaced by unthinkable amounts of hope. I begin chewing on my bottom lip, a feeble attempt to stop the tears, but they well out of my eyes anyway.

Light floods from my skin.

On the screen, walking determinedly towards the camp, is a congregation of around thirty people. I instantly recognise some of the faces from the papers I had found in my father's desk.

The missing.

Th rest of us.

Completely and undeniably alive.

I look up earnestly towards Noah, whose green eyes are also glistening with tears of their own.

He smiles, revealing the dimple upon his scarred, soft cheek.

"Oh stop, you never seen someone cry before?" He asks in a raspy whisper.

Without thinking, I reach my hand up to push his brown, matted hair behind his ear, my eyes not leaving his own.

"Riley?" He says quietly.

"Yeah?"

A pause.

Then he looks away, floppy hair recovering his eyes. "It's almost time to head out there."

"He's right," my father interposes; I had forgotten he had been here all this time. "Riley, are you rested?"

"Yes, I think so."

Noah smiles at me, almost apologetically, unsaid words dressing his eyes. He stands, reaching out a hand, and pulls me up. Before I even realise what is happening, his lips are eminently close to my ear as he whispers "I'm sorry, this wasn't exactly the trip I had planned for us both." Though his words are agile, the feeling of his breath upon my neck sends a river of calm through my body.

"Don't worry about it," I whisper back, revealing the St. Christopher to him. "At least I was safe the whole way here."

He grins. "I have a feeling that safety was due to your own abilities, as opposed to the necklace."

The old woman remains crouched in the corner. "Aren't you coming?" I ask, wondering what on earth she will do while we are gone. Somehow though, I am not worried, because she has already exhibited clearly to us her strength and stubbornness.

"Dear, I'm old, do you think these bones really have the energy to run like your youthful bodies? I'm not immune to age!" I laugh a little. We begin to walk out, but I feel a hand on my shoulder, and she has her other hand on Noah's.

"You weren't born to be quiet, make your words heard."

We will.

Then she looks at me only, and whispers, "Let your light find them all, Riley." And I realise that she doesn't mean my literal light, but my figurative light; the strength within me.

Soon, my father, Noah, and I, are walking through the crowd of the gone, who seem to be waking from the effects of the virus. The snow is calm now, no longer falling from the sky, only remnants on the ground. I really pay attention to what the gone are wearing: white helmets, white gun vests, white boots. Everything is so colourless, and it seems they are prepared for a war that I am sure is approaching, but I am not sure why and how and when. I am fearful—we are fearful—but we still walk through the crowd.

"Endure," I find myself saying under my breath while making sure not to look directly at either my father or Noah. "Verb. To withstand with courage."

"You even read the dictionary, huh?"

"She read a lot down there." My father sounds almost proud, and I guess maybe curiosity is something to be proud of.

"I read it, yes, but I only memorised the best words," I say, taking all my strength not to look Noah in the eyes and smile. We carry on walking, enduring the almost-blank faces that we walk past. I begin picturing these people laughing and smiling and crying and screaming and shouting for all that they love, which is easier to do when their eyes are no longer so vacant.

The buildings around us are all so similar; tall, office like. Much of London, from what I saw at the top of the London Eye, is covered with sections of buildings like this, and we are just in one of many. They are separated by alleys and roads, much of which is filled with the gone who are obeying whatever they have been ordered to do—usually when they are outside, they practise using weapons in secluded areas. My father begins guiding us through the crowd, but his voice trails off, even quieter than it had been from simply trying not to attract any attention. I follow his eyes and see my mother, looking directly at my father. Everything that has ever been between them is there but at the same time it's not, and it breaks my heart. I try to breathe slowly and calm myself, because if my emotion gets too much my body will inevitably release light and that isn't something we need right now.

I walk up to her and look her directly in the eyes, which are glazed over by white like everyone else's. All of me wants to find a way through that barrier, but it isn't possible, not right now. So instead, I brave everything I have and kiss her cheek, whispering 'I love you, Mum'.

As soon as we have walked away, I almost explode in front of my father. "You said she was okay!"

"She is, Ri. The viral effects won't last long on her."

Noah interrupts with, "You lied to us." And though his voice is still calm, it is no longer soft or airy.

"Look," my father begins. "If I hadn't taken Emelia with me, the council would never have believed you were dead Riley, in which case, you would have been taken, or worse. This had to happen." I bite my lip to stop myself from trembling; his voice is focused, dull and dreary.

Almost like the gone's. And then I start walking again, and my father does too but not without repeating, "It won't be long, Emelia." There is now a small amount of hurt within his voice, and I can tell now he is suppressing how much it aches to walk away from her, just to carry on with our mission.

It aches for me too.

Suddenly someone is hugging me from behind, someone small and fragile, sobs escaping her mouth.

"Ebony!" I half shout, half whisper, noticing the attention her sobs are drawing to us but still filled with relieve that she and Liam are here. Liam pats

Noah on the back lightly, nods at my father, and smiles at me. But his face is deliberate and focused, and he says, "We need to find somewhere we can keep lookout for a bit. We have reassured those who are waking, but there is no longer any sign of Thomas and the council, and I'm beginning to get worried. We really gotta figure out what's going on."

"But the gone!" I protest.

"Riley, they could be in serious danger, and there's nothing we can do until we figure out where Thomas is."

"There has to be something."

"Well, there isn't."

My father smiles a little; fond memories appear to be surfacing in his mind.

"It's like you two never got separated."

Liam sighs, and then adds, "Look, just trust me okay."

So, I do.

Noah seems to know a lot of where everything is in this area of London, and I'm not surprised because I am sure before he even met me, he probably spent hours studying it from the London Eye.

"I might regret this," Noah begins, concern shadowing his face. "But I think Liam's right." Liam grimaces before Noah continues.

"And I think I know exactly where to keep lookout."

Liam interrupts. "We need somewhere high up, somewhere we have a good field of view, somewhere—"

"Liam, mate." Noah smirks.

"Yes?"

I start snickering, knowing exactly where Noah means.

"The London Eye."

Liam looks marginally disappointed with himself, but he nods in agreement.

When we reach the Ferris wheel, I am overcome with almost the same amount of awe I had when I was first lead here. Noah smiles at my awe filled face, before instructing us to each take a seat. Ebony, Liam and my father sit on one of the passenger cabins, and I sit on the one following it. Noah runs off, then back, hopping aboard the cabin I am in with a loud thump before it begins to rise. I look above us to make sure the others are okay, and Ebony smiles down at me, long plaits falling aside her face.

Liam reaches in his bag to grab a blanket for her, and I instruct him to wrap her like a caterpillar in a cocoon.

"I am not baby, Riley," she argues, but she is still smiling. I can feel everyone's eyes on us as we laugh, and I know what they are thinking: *It's like they have always been sisters.*

After a while, we agree to take alternate between resting and keeping a lookout.

Ebony and I are the first to rest, but it isn't long before Noah wakes us both. "Noah" Ebony pleads in protest for sleep. "Hey, I know you're tired but you won't hate me when you see this," he whispers softly.

He says it with such excitement and love in his voice that I can't help but ignore the tiredness that consumes me. I begin to sit up and Ebony does too. Noah instructs us to both close our eyes. "You ready, Ebony?"

"Yes," she says, pure excitement in her voice. It is a beautiful thing, to see how she has changed from pure fear to pure wonder in the last few hours. Noah sometimes tells me it's because of me that she has found her curiosity towards the world again, but I know it is also him.

Noah lifts his hands delicately from my eyes, and Liam takes his hands away from Ebony's eyes. The grey clouds that had once crowded the sky have completely disappeared to reveal the Milky Way, and I don't think I have ever been in more awe than I am now.

It's now that I notice how much warmer it is out here all of a sudden. True, the coolness is still present, but it is no more than what I have always imagined a normal early morning breeze would be.

In all the whiteness that was once around us, the sky is now filled with purple and blue and orange and green, and about approximately two-hundred and fifty-billion stars make themselves at home there in that one galaxy, our galaxy.

I hold my hand out as though I can reach them, and Ebony does the same, standing on the very tips of her toes to try. I wonder if she has ever seen anything like this before, but from the look on her face it's quite clear she hasn't.

"You like it?" Noah asks us both, still staring up at the sky. I think about all the nights I lay Underneath, looking out the tiny crack above my head and convincing myself I could maybe see a star, that it was within my grasp even though I was not even Above. Now, I am sure that I wasn't seeing stars. That doesn't even come close to what I am witnessing now; it is as if the world has stopped for a second to show us its canvas in all its clarity, God's canvas, right here before our eyes.

Even though the stars are of the same value, I know for a fact not one is identical to another. Some will be molten-gold and others will be solar-yellow, some will be flickering and others will be flashing. It's as though each star is a beacon of hope for all the gone, all of the broken souls.

Ebony lays down and we watch her staring at them like she belongs in the sky, then as the reflection of the stars is hidden by her eyelids and she is once again fast asleep.

"Is it your turn to rest?" I yawn, looking over at Noah who is sat huddled up next to me. I want to stay in this moment completely, forever, but we have to save the Above first, and Noah knows that too.

"Not yet," he says, and I am questioning that because it means he has something else that he wants to do.

With Noah, there's always something else.

"I love a lotta people, Riley," he whispers. I wait for him to continue, searching his green eyes earnestly."

"The thing is," he begins, "there are different types of love. I was with my mother once, before the storm, and she told me one day I'd fall in love. You heard that saying? About the type of love you fall for?"

I trace my mind for books I have read, and the dictionary enters it.

"Love. Noun. An intense feeling of deep affection. That's love, right?"

"Yeah, for sure. But there is also the kinda love that gives you goose bumps, a rapid pulse every time you see that person." He cringes at his own voice a little, but I listen to each and every word in all seriousness.

Wait.

One.

Minute.

Yes, I am definitely not allergic to Noah; my racing heart, goosebumps, everything had been entirely the opposite. All the forces of the world around us seem to be pushing us together as though we are magnets, and my heart will not stop pounding.

"There's a difference between 'I love you' and 'love you' you know." I know, because the 'I' has made all the difference in any slightly romantic book I have ever read.

"And, Riley," even just him saying my name makes the whole world spin and there's nothing I can do to stop it.

He inhales, and breathes out slowly, "I love you."

The same nervousness that I had when I first met him surfaces again and I say, "Um, are you sure?"

My stupid mouth.

But he laughs, and then I laugh, and then we are back to being quiet because otherwise we will wake everyone.

"I am two-hundred and fifty-billion percent sure, if not a little more than that," I smile, and he will know that my blush is no longer because of the cold.

"I think I love you too," and I go to say more but I can't because his lips are on mine, warmer with love than anything I have ever felt in my entire life. His hands go to my cheeks and they are warm too, and suddenly I am glowing with light and it is like I have the entire Milky Way floating in my body. I try to apologise for my immune system's eccentric reaction to the stronger viral injection, but I can't because his lips are still there. And then he lets go and kisses the tip of my nose, my head, my cheek.

My father always said he didn't think I would ever get to feel this kind of love because everyone up here was gone, but he didn't realise I would fall in love with someone who was going to help me save this world.

For just this moment though, while we wait for the air to warm even more, I stay in Noah's arms and let the sun rise fully.

It is the best night of my entire life.

Chapter Seventeen

Riley

It isn't long before Ebony and I have to wake the others from their rest. We are met by unnerving voice, once again surging through megaphones across the city.

"Congratulations. You have a mind of your own. But if you fail to fight for us, we have no choice but to deprive you of your existence."

"Crap. The virus effects…" Noah whispers, as I grab a hold of him to remain calm and keep from exploding with fear.

"He's going to hurt them. Mum's down there!" Liam screams. He begins to climb down the ferris wheel, fearless.

"Mum…" Ebony echoes, her voice small and forlorn.

I know they are fearful, desperation filling their every bone. But I have to interrupt them. "Wait!" I cry. "If we don't know location, there's no way on earth we'll be able to stop him."

Although they don't want to wait, they know I'm right. The whole reason we came up here in the first place was to look out where he is hiding.

Liam ruthlessly hangs on to the outside of his passenger cabin by one arm. He uses the other to search, narrowing his eyes. The rest of us do the same.

There's no sight of him.

I try to think of somewhere he would be able to speak through the megaphones, somewhere you might not expect.

The stadium.

"The stadium," Noah says, speaking my thoughts aloud. "He's inside the stadium."

Noah grabs my hand tight, and we all begin to abseil down the wheel. When we land, we quicken our pace, knowing exactly where we are headed.

It turns out the missing know exactly where to head too. Soon, we are our own army, running together with the new, clean air flowing through our lungs.

Once a small mass of birds, but now a flock, flying stubbornly towards our enemy.

To get to the stadium, we have to run through the crowd of the no-longer-gone. The daring join us, others watch, disconcerted.

We have no time to stop.

Which is why I am startled when Ebony does.

My father continues to pace forward, but I pull Noah back, and Liam also halts.

Ebony stands as still as stone. Her eyes are wide, and when I follow her gaze, I glimpse a woman in the far distance, looking desperately around her, chanting the same name over and over again.

"Ebony!"

"It's her mother," says Liam, not taking his eyes off her.

"Ebony, I know what you are thinking, but we can't waste any time, it's too dangerous. We have to go, now." Liam tries to tug at her arm, but she refuses to move a muscle.

"I'd risk everything for her…" she whispers.

"EBONY!" Liam is shouting now, angrily. "Riley, talk to her. She'll only listen to you."

I try to grab a hold of Ebony's hand, try to keep my own hand, the entire ground, from trembling.

And that's when she looks into my eyes regretfully, desperate.

"You will let me go to my mother! あなたは私を母のところへ行かせます!"

Everything is black for a moment, and it is like someone has taken control of my body as I watch, internally, unable to do anything but cry out within.

"Okay," I whisper externally. Internally, a thousand different thoughts swarm through my mind.

It is hard to see through the eyes of someone else, but sometimes you do not even need to look into their eyes to feel what they are feeling. Psychology states strong feelings make our bodies do things we cannot always control. I cannot see through Ebony's eyes, but I can feel her desperation, and I can feel the adrenaline that courses through her veins in that moment. I can feel her tears rolling down my cheeks, I can feel the wind that she runs through after pushing away my arm.

"Ebony!" I want to shout, but it comes out as a croak. A thousand 'Ebony's do not echo like a thousand 'Riley's' used to Underneath. They fade into the air and they refuse to make a sound.

"She can come with us, it'll be okay!" she shouts behind her without looking back, her eyes evermore fixated on her mother, but not upon the gun a guard nearby holds.

"Ebony!" Liam shouts, "You don't under—"

She runs even further into the crowd, screaming at the top of her weak lungs, "Mum! Mama! I'm here, I'm here!" Now she is looking all around her, silent apart from her quick breaths.

I cannot see through her eyes, but I can feel her desperation.

The trance fades, and I can speak in a whisper. "Liam, Liam, you have known her longer. You know her. You can talk her out of this, right? Has she ever done anything like this before?"

"Actually, you know her better."

"What?"

"You know her better, Riley. You make her brave. Your curiosity towards the world, your light, it made her realise there is good still left in it."

"You are blaming me for the fact she is risking her life?"

"No, I am saying you gave her more life than she has ever known. You're the only one who can save her, Riley, you're stronger than me and you know it. Please."

Ebony is still looking around. I have to blink twice to confirm that the crowd is slowly moving closer to her, partly because of the snow falling in front of my eyes and partly because of my tiredness, which I am quite certain will cause me to hallucinate soon enough.

"Young girl..." a voice echoes through the whole crowd.

The gunman.

"I would stay very, very still if I were you."

But Ebony does not stay still. She cannot seem to slow her breath, and she cannot control her head which keeps turning in every direction possible. Eventually, she locates her mother, but although she is now only staring at her, it does not stop the newfound panic that seems to escape her and cause her to shake excessively. Still, she raises her head high and maintains eye contact with her mother.

Around her, the buildings seem a lot bigger. The people seem a lot stronger. The wind blows a little faster.

She is so different to me, but she is our people. She is my *sister*. Why am I not running to help her? It's as though I am rooted in the ground. Perhaps I say this aloud, because Liam looks at me with warning and sadness that I have never witnessed from him before. He does not want me to move, but my heart says otherwise. Yet still, my feet are rooted evermore.

Silently, I will them to move.

They do not.

The trance is still affecting me.

"Mama," she half whispers, half shouts, somehow loud enough for us to hear her. I watch intently. The loyalty she holds for this woman, these people, is seemingly everlasting. When she addresses her mother, she is addressing the entire crowd.

"It's going to be okay." For a moment, I think I see a tear roll down the gunman's cheek. I think I see his hand shake; his gun drops slightly.

Perception is misleading when you are exhausted.

Instead, the gun begins to rise again, directly pointed at Ebony. She does not flinch. She does not raise her hands to cover her face, or try to run. Instead, she takes a small step forward.

"Ebony, go back."

My feet are no longer rooted in the ground.

"*Riley!* I can't lose you again!" Liam shouts, changing his mind, from behind me, his voice the echo of the voice he held when he was a young boy.

"You didn't lose me," I shout back. "I lost you. You'll never lose me. I love you."

I feel running footsteps behind me; Noah and Liam, refusing to leave a soldier behind.

My feet are bruised. I am pretty sure one of them is broken. But it doesn't matter, because everyone here is broken. And I want to unbreak them.

"Ebony," I whisper as I run, her name repeated in sync with my racing heart. She turns to me, smiling.

And then time stops.

The gun is pointed.

The trigger is pulled.

It flies through the air like a dagger.

I don't stop running.

I try to push her out the way.

I am holding her.

She is covered in crimson.

"I failed to save my people?" she asks, looking up at me.

"No, no, no, no." I put my hand carefully behind her neck and do not even try to stop my tears. But I forage a small smile. "You did not fail. You are the bravest person I know. Because you didn't just try to help your mother. You didn't just help the gone. You have helped all of humanity. Always."

"Have I helped you, my sister? My brothers, Noah, Liam?"

"Yes."

She smiles. "We are all so different." She laughs slightly, then coughs. "Noah is funny and loving, and Liam is stubborn but strong, and you…" she pauses, takes a breath, "you are everything a sister should be."

"And so are you." I sob a little, but my smile still remains.

"It is not beautiful?"

"Hmm?" I can't speak anymore. I hold her and don't let go, watching intently as she continues to smile a little, even though it's causing her too much effort, too much pain.

"Humanity, without the virus."

"It is."

Noah is by me within seconds, whispering with hurt and desperation and concern, all at once. "We gotta go." He pauses to look down at Ebony, and it hurts me even more because a heavy sob catches in his throat. I can feel his pain when he rests his hand on my shoulder; his love for Ebony is flooding out of him as though he has been stabbed in the chest.

"Okay."

And now Liam is here too, not even trying to hold back his loud cries of grief as he picks up Ebony who is now no more than a mannequin, a shell. His tears glisten as they cover Ebony's face, shoulder's, entire body. I gulp and then we are all running again, knowing we cannot stop. I know Thomas is watching from somewhere; he probably has access to his communication device, he could tell us to stop, but he doesn't. He doesn't say a thing, because not even a dictating member of the government can find words to fill this abyss.

I haven't stopped walking until now because I have been trying to numb the pain by exhausting my body. Even though it feels as though I've trekked through half of London, the pain is not going. My father told me once when people have painful operations, they are given medication and injections that numb the hurt, but there is nothing that can numb what feels like my heart being ripped out of my chest.

As we run. I can feel the gunman trying to shoot at us.

But he is defenceless against my fury, which rips through the ground, my power throwing him brutally against a building.

Noah turns to face me and Liam, lips trembling, and I grasp a hold of his hand to calm myself.

Liam calls out to the both of us "Go ahead with the rest of them. I need to stop, to put her down. I can't help you much, anyway; I have nothing." Within moments he is gone, running in the opposite direction. We don't look back, because if we did, we would never continue forward.

Noah and I must stop after another mile or so of running.

I look up and he is opposite, staring at me, eyes unmoving. It's as though he is trying to read my mind, and I am suddenly self-conscious of my tangled hair blowing in the wind, the blood on my sleeves where I held Ebony, the weakness in my eyes, and I want to look away from him, at the flattened grass, but I can't. It is eerily quiet, and we are bruised and battered and speechless. It hurts to look at his tear-streaked cheeks, and it hurts even more that he is looking at mine.

We stand unintentionally in sync, turn and walk at the same time, his left and my right. He grabs my head and puts it on his chest and wipes my tears and I reach up and wipe his, and he holds me until we both can't cry anymore. He kisses my head with his soft, peeling lips and I let him. I look down and my chest is glowing, glowing, glowing, it is the light that only love and sadness all at once can bring.

Among all this darkness, I will not let the light go.

People are crying everywhere, children are screaming for their parents, parents are screaming for their children. Husbands push through crowds for their wives and some bow on the floor praying. It is clear they remember everything, but now they have control and the years that they have lost are presenting themselves clearer than ever before. Suddenly, the air is a little too warm, my hand brushing my face to wipe away the beads of sweat building on my forehead. I see Ebony's mother, and my heart stops inside of my chest. She is sitting by a wall away from the panicked crowds of people, hugging her knees and looking far more vulnerable than anyone here. Silent tears roll down her cheeks, but she doesn't wipe them away, she just lets them run their course. Her hands are shaking, trembling beyond control.

I push my way through the crowd, ignoring Noah's hands upon my shoulders. I am past the point of caring for my safety.

"Hey," I whisper, walking up to her and crouching down slowly.

She doesn't look up, instead, she just whispers, "You were with her, did you treat her well?"

"Yes, ma'am, I did." I call her 'ma'am' to show her I respect her as a human being.

"I don't deserve that, I do not deserve to be called 'ma'am'. I should've have fought the virus, should have helped her."

"There is nothing you could have done," I say, my voice hoarse. "What is your name?" I ask her.

"Yua."

"That's a beautiful name," I whisper.

"It is supposed to mean 'binding love', but I do not feel bound; the only person I have ever loved is gone." Her last words get caught in her throat, a tear simultaneously rolling down her cheek.

It hurts to look at her because her eyes are exactly like Ebony's; big and dark and full of horrible memories, but also some beautiful ones too. I make sure to look directly at them though because she needs to know I am listening to her.

"My friends and I are going to try and bring love, Yua. We want you to help us."

"Young girl, what do you think I can do? My baby, she's gone." She loses it, and her face becomes a melancholy flood. I reach over and wipe her tears away slightly.

"She's not gone, not really. She's here and she's watching you, and you know what she will want you to do?"

"What?"

"Ebony would've wanted you to fight with us the right way. With your voice."

Noah holds out his hand to her, and he is not ordering her to take our help but he is simply knocking on the door, waiting for her to answer. Thankfully, she does, and I sigh a breath of relief because I don't want her to go too, not like her daughter. She knows that she can't go, that she shouldn't, and although there is an exhaustible amount of pain soaring through her eyes it's clear she is going to

126

fight through it. She always has been a fighter, deep down, and it's not that hard to be able to see that in her.

"Hold courage, and don't be afraid," I'll never get bored of saying these words; they shine through me brighter than any light possibly could.

"I have lost my family," she proclaims, sadness filling every inch of her heart.

"You haven't lost all of your family. We are still here, and we aren't going anywhere. We promise." It's a difficult promise to make and one even I'm not sure we can keep, not after what happened with Ebony. But it's a promise that I will do everything in my power to maintain.

Yua stands and I help her up with my father, brother and Noah. She is very weak; I cannot comprehend how it feels to suddenly have your body back after a manmade virus has claimed it for so many years.

All we can do is give her love and light and healing and loyalty, everything humanity should hold and will hold again.

I hope it's just a matter of time before everything changes.

Liam

I sit down on one side of the river, right back where we had been, by the London Eye. Around the water there is somehow some colourful vegetation that has established its place around the gates, despite the previously cold conditions.

In this moment, I care about nothing but Ebony.

A sister I didn't even realise I had for so long.

Her dark cheeks still feel warm to touch, but her neck is heavy against my hands.

I haven't cried in fifteen years. Not until now.

In this moment, I am extremely aware of how sacred living is, especially in people like Ebony. I count the times our souls – mine, hers, Noah's – sang together, smiled together, survived together. She gave Noah and I a reason to carry on, to keep fighting and to refuse the tight grip of the government.

In her reddened coat pocket is her soft toy. The toy I always told her to dispose of, a sign she was immune.

I gasp through my tears as I pick it up, adjust her open palms so that she is clutching the toy for one last time.

Then my tears cover her face, and I close my eyes in agony.

Through my eyelids, I can see a bright, overwhelming glisten. I open my eyes to glinting tears; a glimmering blanket covering Ebony completely.

And then it happens.

Her small palm touches my face. "Brother." She inhales sharply, coughs.

My eyes widen with unimaginable disbelief.

"Brother, you healed me."

Then we are both laughing and crying hysterically, tears rolling down our cheeks as I hold her and protect her.

"My sister. I will not let anything happen to you again."

Chapter Eighteen

We run back out into the crowd and Noah, the missing and I are screaming at the top of our lungs for them to listen, to calm down, but they will not. I can't judge them for it, they've been through a lot more than words can describe and it's only now that they are allowed to react to it. Fifteen years of pain and restriction is now surfacing from within them, but it is happening all at once and they are going to get themselves killed.

These people—who once wore pristine white uniforms and were so orderly and willing to use weapons—are now tearing at their uniforms, staring at their weapons as though they are already looking at a dead person.

"Please!" I shout, and my throat hurts. "Please, just listen, we can help you!" I'm not exactly sure why I say that, but it's probably true that we are the ones whose minds are not *as* confused as theirs right now.

My body starts to glow a little, the emotion triggering the light.

That's it.

I let my emotion flow through me completely, and with that so does the light. A few people stop and stare, silence filling them, but there are too many and I cannot do this on my own.

Noah gets the idea, asking some people to come close to him. He puts his hand on their shoulders and I watch as they literally feel his calm pour into them, their hearts relaxing and warming all at the same time. I marvel at him, at the impact we are making.

One of them screams, "Why did you do this? Why did you take away our identities?" Every single person here is different and it's crazy how only a day ago they all seemed to be exactly the same.

"Attention! Right now! All of you," Thomas's voice blares from a megaphone across the entire area. I'd imagine it is being broadcast across the whole of England, especially if these riots are happening everywhere.

We are nearing the stadium, and Noah nods at me, indicating we have to go in. We slip through the crowd with the rest of the missing, listening to his voice as we run.

"Years ago, I don't know if you remember, but there were people *attacking* us. It wasn't just our country. Anywhere the attackers could strike, they would; concerts, famous buildings, you name it. They began the war. Not me, them." The sound of stress in his voice is building, although I can't help but think it was him that brought this stress upon himself.

"This virus made you all the same. If we are all the same, we can all kill the attackers. If not, then most of you would have appealed against the cause to, essentially, save your *lives*. I'm going to give you all a final warning, a count of three. Pick up your weapons, resume your training, or you will be devoid of existence!" I look around me, and it is unbelievable because people are actually starting to pick up their weapons again, as though everything inside of them is broken and they have no choice.

We can't let this happen.

Noah grabs a fallen gun from the floor.

We run into the stadium, see his back as he stands on the stage, a microphone connected to all megaphones gripped firmly in his hands.

The rest of the missing remain outside, and I hear one of them scream. "For our people!"

"Three," Thomas hums, not realising we are behind him. Another person in the crowd starts to whisper it before they become as loud as the first, and this encourages several others to harmonise alongside them. This is a chain reaction that cannot be undone, a minority coalition in which everyone is agreeing to be different.

There may have been attacks on the Above, on our city, but we cannot become our own biggest enemy. We cannot condescend to that level because we are our own people.

"Two." Thomas's mouth gets closer to the microphone.

"FOR OUR PEOPLE!" the chant continues.

"*One,*" Noah whispers, before Thomas gets the chance.

He turns to face us, and Noah holds up the gun, aiming directly at Thomas.

Thomas smirks, begins to clap slowly. He starts to walk towards us.

"I wouldn't walk a step further if I were you," Noah warns.

"Ah, Noah Jordan, we both know you won't pull that trigger. There is far too much love within you; one of the main reasons the virus needed to affect you most. Of course, that didn't quite work out as planned now, did it?"

"Maybe not for you," Noah remarks, adjusting a firmer grip upon the gun.

"Go on," Thomas gestures towards the gun, towards Noah's shaking hands. "I'd like to see you try."

Without warning, my father runs through the doors, plucking the gun from Noah's hands.

"Ah, James, my old friend. I'm so happy you could—"

Before he can finish, James pulls the trigger, and I jump back in shock. Although the gunshot only fired once, the sound echoes through my ears a thousand times as I watch Thomas fall to the ground.

It's as though I am watching Ebony get shot all over again, crimson covering her small, fragile body.

Thomas looks down in dismay, grabbing a hold of his chest.

Noah and I try to run towards him, but my father stops us.

"We have no time. He's already instructed…" He cannot continue his sentence through a sudden on burst of coughs.

Suddenly, we are all coughing; smoke consumes our lungs and our eyes are numb beyond belief.

"Tear gas," my father finishes between his own coughs, and he gestures for us to run with him, outside and into the crowd.

I spot Yua and call for her to take cover. Yua shakes her head in protest. "I need to stay, to help fix their wounds."

"You can't fix their wounds until your own wounds are fixed," Noah says this just loud enough for her to hear, and near the end of the sentence his own words fade into the smoke and coughing and pain.

We try to resist helping Thomas as we gather as many people inside the stadium as we can, shutting the door behind us. The missing direct others to elsewhere. My father rips off bits of his jacket for each of us to breathe into. Small amounts of oxygen make way into my body and it's strange knowing how to breathe again. I wonder if this is how the gone felt after they became un-gone.

Tears continue to fall from my eyes but I don't think it's the tear gas anymore. Or if it is, then that's only contributing to it. Most of the tears are full of emotion which I can't seem to shake, and I feel like I should be doing something; I feel entirely hopeless.

131

My body is hurling itself up but Noah hurls me right back down again because I cannot stop coughing, and I let him because it takes too much strength to pull away. All my strength goes into crying even though I don't will it to. I can't help it, instead, my emotion just takes over.

"Why—" I cough, try again. "Why would he do something like this? To Ebony." I am talking about Thomas, and the entirety of the council, all swayed with brutality. My father shakes his head a little too vigorously. "This is why Thomas has to be killed."

Thomas remains in the corner of the room, reaching out desperately.

"Are we not as bad as him, now?" Noah asks. I know in my heart he would never have pulled the trigger.

My father sighs, opens his mouth to speak through the coughing, and then stops himself.

Then I see her.

Carried upon his shoulders, clasping securely on to his neck.

Alive.

Breathing, as much as she can breathe through the gas.

"EBONY!" I scream, a flurry of tears pouring down on to my coat, still covered in her blood.

She was dead…

I run up to her, and so does Noah. We grab Liam and Ebony and hold them in our arms, tighter than we have ever held them before.

"I missed you." Ebony whispers, looking up at me with her huge, dark-brown eyes.

"How…" Noah says softly.

"Turns out it's not just me I can heal," Liam answers Noah before looking across the room at Thomas, who is trying to crawl over to us, cries of agony escaping his throat between gasps of breath.

We pull back, because Ebony's wide eyes become fixated on someone else.

Her mother.

They are a mirror image of one another, depicting love, relief, and the need for each other's embrace. Within seconds Ebony is huddled in her mother's arms, clinging to her steadfastly.

We take a second to cherish the hope that is present in this moment, but then we are taken back to our surroundings.

Everyone is still coughing, still hunched over, trying to breathe. But the gas is wearing off, and now the council are no longer receiving orders from Thomas, they seem uncertain on what moves to make.

"What're we gonna do when the gas has diminished?"

"We have to separate, that's for sure," my father says.

"What? We are a minority, how are we gonna stop this mess if we make our small minority an even smaller minority?" Liam is protesting aloud, and I don't make an attempt to stop him. Noah doesn't either, and that's how you know he agrees because most of the time I've been with them the two disagree a whole lot.

"You don't understand, Liam. We are no longer a minority. Take a look out there. The council are practically nothing without orders, not compared to us." And we do. There are people now hugging and trying to fix each other's wounds. In fact, I can see Yua and Ebony have made her way out there too, fixing the wounds of children around Ebony's age, not wanting anything to happen to them like it did to her. None of us noticed that they had gone in between our coughing and spluttering for air. I watch them for a moment fixedly, standing in awe.

In that moment, I long for my mother's embrace.

Which is when I see her, searching the crowd. No longer held captive by the effects of the virus.

She is not alone, but with a man and a woman, both of which appear to be searching for someone.

Their sons and daughters.

"Mum! Dad!" Noah cries.

I cannot bring myself to speak. I just let my mother hold us, me and Liam, both her children again in her arms after fifteen years.

"Hey." Liam croaks, looking up at her with tear-streaked cheeks.

"Hey, stranger," my mother responds, kissing his forehead. "I'm so glad you're safe."

My father's voice brings me back into our conversation. He says the words while putting a hand on my mother's shoulder.

I cannot help but remember how he let her succumb to the effects of the virus.

"Some of us should go help around the crowds, make sure everybody is okay and healthy. This virus—" he pauses at the word virus, guilt flooding through him again before he continues. "This virus has been alive in these people for fifteen years, and their bodies have adjusted to the cold weather. It's likely a lot of their immune systems will be in shock, so our main priority is keeping them all well."

"The rest of us can then tell the crowd we need to stand up for our beliefs, not hide away from them. None of us were born to be silent; especially not you three."

"Even if we got this crowd to listen to us, we'd need the whole of the Above to listen, and that's just not possible," I argue My father is quick to counter-argue.

"Ri, have you ever heard of live television?"

"Of course. I remember it."

"Well, I know some people who can make that work."

I remember watching it as a toddler, the news presenters and their accounts of what was going on in the world around them. But I don't think I can speak on television, not on behalf of everyone in the Above. My voice isn't loud enough for that; it won't make a difference in all the chaos. But my father doesn't even wait for me to respond before getting up and gesturing for Liam and my mother to go with him.

"You, Emelia and I are going to help the people out there, you hear me, Son?"

"I hear you." Liam doesn't protest, doesn't hold a look of insignificance upon his face anymore. I want him to feel the need to speak, to take my place, and he sees the discomfort in my eyes when he says "It's you who needs to do this, Riley."

"Noah, you stay with Riley. You protect my daughter," My father says. It's an order, not a question.

"Yes, sir," Noah salutes my father and I can't help but let laughter escape my lips. All too quickly though, the present situation comes back to me and the laughter is simultaneously dissipated.

I take a breath. In a way, none of us want to do anything because we are fearful our anything will not account to anything successful, but rather something very unsuccessful.

We won't know until we try.

I stand, which seems to be the signal for everyone else to stand too.

"Wait," my father ruffles around in his pocket.

He presents five masks, which should help us make it to our chosen locations outside.

It turns out Thomas used live broadcasting regularly to communicate with everyone in authority across the country. But when we reach the people who are in control of all this technological equipment, they are more than willing to help without us even needing to explain. I wonder how long they have wanted out of Thomas's barbaric dictatorship, but it seems like it's been quite a long while.

We watch as they get prepared to switch on the cameras, instructing them to capture a large stand with a microphone. This is where my father instructed Noah and I to head to, preparing to speak to the whole of the Above.

When the cameras are all ready, we thank the people who helped us, adjust our masks and head towards the stand. There is, of course, no longer any wind, but it feels like there is with all the panic in the crowds. It gusts over us a lot stronger than any air could; a tempest greater than the one before.

Two flashes from the camera on the opposite wall – the signal – and I need to talk. My heart is pounding and I really, really do not want to do this. But Noah takes my hand and squeezes it and there it is, the river of calm. And now, while my heart is still pounding, it is bursting with comfort from him and from my family, wherever they are. I need to do this for all of them, even if it takes all my strength.

One flash, red and quick and bright. It draws the attention of the crowds and they look at it curiously. Another flash, the exact same. No more flashes, that's the two we agreed on, that's the signal.

I gulp and hold my breath.

Noah helps me up on to the stand and I am trying not to shake.

"Courage, it's me, don't be afraid," I hear the voice loud and clear and I think this is maybe an auditory hallucination because I cannot see where it is coming from. In the distance though, I am almost certain I see the doe I found when I first entered the Above: the first sign of hope in this desolate world. She tilts her head up and stares directly at me, challenging me again. She looks around and she is curious to see what I can do; her eyes are brown and filled with wonder. Noah is watching me patiently.

I tap the microphone. Noah nods once.

"Um, hello—" I cough a little. There are eyes on me everywhere, even across the entirety of the Above, but this isn't so bad. I let my heart do the talking.

"My name is Riley. I was immune to this virus that changed you all. I was also one of the people who has helped to stop it," Noah squeezes my hand again, encouraging me to carry on, and so I do.

135

"I don't know what you all believed in before the virus took control of your minds. God? A higher being, a source of creation. But I believe in something, and I believe that something made each and every one of us to be unique, to have authentic souls that can relish in the wonder that is life. I am so sorry this was taken away from you.

"This virus you were all exposed to is one which was man made. It was created so that each and every one of you would willingly use violence, with no opposition, to kill attackers who, if you remember, attacked this country and many others because they wanted everyone to hold the exact same belief as them. Life doesn't work like that though." My eyes close. "If we all use violence, we are all as bad as them. If we all become the same – robotic and lifeless – we are giving them what they want. Thomas led us to becoming our own biggest enemy."

I have every single person's attention in the area, all their eyes are focused on me.

Curiosity appears again. She bows her head and then runs off into the distance, as though she is satisfied with my words.

I push the microphone to Noah and let him speak now. It is beginning to get late; the sun is falling in the sky and everything is a mixture of colours, an assortment of shades brighter than I have ever seen. Noah's voice trails across the crowd and into the sky like a bird flying gracefully. Compassion fills his every word.

"We are gonna fight this battle the right way. That's staying strong in our beliefs, not ever wavering. We were made the way we are for a reason, and as long as that way is filled with goodness than who are we to let anyone take it away from us? You embrace every single hair on your head—that's right, even the grey ones," a few laughs emerge from the crowd, "you love what you wanna love, feel what you wanna feel. Let courage and let love be your guidance, and tell fear to be on its way."

In the distance, Liam and my father look up and smile. Liam is bandaging up a young boy, and my father is holding my mother in his arms. I spot the old woman in the distance, and she raises both her palms to the sky. I do the same, and it feels sort of out of place until everyone starts doing it.

We are all united.

Our palms almost touch the golden sky and we let it surround us. Noah is the last to raise his palms because he is looking to everyone else first, making sure they're okay and with us and safe.

But Thomas refuses to let us leave without one final breath of warning. The megaphones begin to echo as weak words escape his lips.

"None of you realise what you are doing, you'll regret this!"

And then we hear his drop to the floor, the last of his excruciating pain diminishing as he breathes his final breath.

The sky is filled with stars now, just like the ones Noah showed Ebony and I. I start crying, a mixture of emotions overwhelming me.

"We are fighting!" I scream back.

That's when I hear it.

The reason Thomas had created his army.

The bomb makes a large *bang* in the far distance. It doesn't reach anybody here, but there is silence despite.

"How are you going to fight now, then?" Though Thomas is not with us, I can hear his voice internally, challenging me evermore. Another *bang* sounds in the distance. They aren't extremely powerful, but they are enough to cause serious damage if they get close enough.

I look at my father in the crowd for guidance, and it seems like he has a plan, so I call him over and up here as fast as I possibly am able to. He reaches Noah and me in no time at all, and he is quick to speak.

"There is shelter for protection from these attacks just behind us, big enough for many of you. Parents, get your children in there and anybody who is vulnerable as fast as you possibly can. There will be people there to help you and get you anything you need as soon as possible. Everyone else needs to stand behind this stand. I will be grabbing protective clothing and I advise you to keep it on at all times. We cannot run from this any longer, so when the time comes you all need to trust me and follow what I say. Does anyone hold any opposition to this plan? If you do please say now." No one says a word. "Okay, let's get moving."

Noah grabs my hand and begins to lead me with the others to shelter, but I stop him.

"I'm staying out here, Noah."

"It's too dangerous."

"You and I both know that we are the only people who can end this war. Are you staying out here?"

"Yeah, but—"

"Then I'm staying out here too."

My stubbornness is a barricade and I'm not letting it down. I understand that he wants to protect me, and it fills my heart, but I refuse to leave these people outside all alone.

"Riley?" My father says my name before I move a muscle.

"Yes?"

"Stay safe out there." And though I hear the concern in his voice that is that of a loving father's, I also know he is perceiving me as a weapon, a means to fight back. "I will be safe," I whisper.

"Okay."

"Okay?"

"Yes, Riley, okay. But you listen to my every word out here, you hear me?"

"I hear you."

"Good."

We help people inside first, getting them to the shelter which, thankfully, isn't too far away. Every so often it sounds like there is another strike nearby, but I can't be sure because my head hurts so much and I wouldn't be surprised if it is just the pounding. Usually, I can tell when there is actually a strike, because it is a lot louder and everybody winces a little.

Once enough people are inside, the rest of us walk out with our heads high. This doesn't mean nerves don't fill every inch of our bones, but the air is in our favour and the sky is beautiful and every single star is shining down on us.

When we are sure everyone is in shelter, we return back to the stand. My father, my mother, Liam, Noah, Ebony, Yua, and I; a protective shield. I would laugh at how sweet it is, or hug them for it. But none of us do anything other than wait, protective clothing and our prayers embracing us.

Noah leans slightly closer to me, just enough so that our arms are almost touching. I let him because his closeness helps.

I wonder if the entire cosmos is afraid like I am at this very moment, but maybe this year is pointless. Why should anybody fear the future or the past? Both essentially only exist in no place but imagination or memory, and neither of those have to be a threat if you don't let them.

Bang.

We wince.

Bang.

That one is a little closer, and half of us duck.

They are coming closer, and my body trembles, and therefore so do my surroundings. Fear soars through me, as well as the need to protect my family.

"Rifles," Noah whispers. "They're carrying rifles."

Dust blows around in the air, and our surroundings begin to look dark, eerie.

But in despite of this, I try and turn my fear to courage. There must be a reason my father wanted to keep me hidden for fifteen years, an evaluation of my extraordinary, immune mind.

I look over at him, and he is staring directly at me.

Waiting.

I close my eyes and picture light. It begins as a mass of embers, then transitions into a flame.

I hear the attackers pull their triggers, all simultaneously.

I squeeze my eyes tighter, gripping tightly on to Liam and Noah's hands, and they do the same to the others.

The flame becomes a fire.

I open my eyes.

The bullets are flying towards us, but they stop directly in front of our faces as each and every one of us flinch.

"What the…" Liam starts, awestruck.

"It's Riley," Noah exclaims, staring at me, gobsmacked.

In front of us is a translucent, glowing shield. My energy is faltering, and it takes all of my strength to keep the shield up, feeding from my emotions.

The bullets bounce off the barrier mercilessly and all at once, firing back towards the direction of their shooters.

I drop the shield, and with the shield I fall to the ground. My ears are ringing, and I think I'm on my back because I can see the sky in a blur of colours and smoke. There are flames everywhere and I want to throw up because my lungs are intoxicated. I've never felt this sort of physical pain, the kind where your lungs are on fire.

Someone is maybe calling my name, but I'm not sure because of the ringing. It is also very hard to distinguish whether the ringing is coming from my head or the distance.

Liam is trying to heave me up, and I let him even though it hurts a lot. As soon as I am standing and blink enough to see, I scream. It sounds horrible, like I am broken and shattered.

He whispers "Noah was hit. Before the shield." I turn and see him lying there. His complexion is ashen where it was once glowing, picturesque, golden, and stamped unevenly, perfectly with his one dimple.

"Noah, please..." I am crying, I can't help it. My face is tear streaked and smoke stained and everything in between.

I put my head on his chest and I can't feel it beating, can't hear it among the chaos.

Maybe it isn't beating at all.

The noises everywhere engulf me, rendering any logical thought so that all I am left with is a dominating, profound darkness.

My father and Liam haul Noah up and half pull, half carry him towards the nearest doors to safety. I am reluctant to let them go, but I try to entrust Noah in Liam's hands. My father tells me he knows I am worried, but that there are a lot of injured people who need help.

In the near distance, I spot Yua on the floor, her head bleeding. Ebony is leant over her, in tears.

It looks bad.

"Yua? I need you to speak to me, okay, say something?" It feels like I can't breathe.

I had not prepared myself for harm to come to more people. Especially not this.

Especially not Ebony's mother.

I continue to hold my hand under her neck, just like it had been with Ebony.

I begin to cry all over again.

She's already stone cold.

"I think she's been gone a while, sweetheart," the words catch in my mother's throat. She wipes away a tear.

I nod because there is nothing else I can do. Words physically will not enter my throat, will not leave my lips. I could say a million words, each one equal in cadence and sentiment. But no words I have ever read, have ever learnt, none will bring Yua back to Ebony. My mother pulls me and Ebony – who screams in agony – into an embrace and I remember how much I missed her hugs.

"I can't keep going," I whisper into her chest.

Liam

"We have to," I do as my father says, but it's so hard. My entire body aches and I've thrown up consistently, even though I physically don't have anything to throw up any longer.

After an eternity, we've reached safety. Crowds inside move for us so we can walk Noah in and rest him against a wall; the closest thing to a bed we have.

He is conscious, and unsurprisingly the first thing he asks is "Is everyone safe?" followed quickly by "Wait, where's Riley?"

When he realises Riley isn't with us, he looks like he is in more pain from her absence than he is from his injuries. I understand this completely. But right now, I am concerned about his injuries, because his head is bleeding—though the cut doesn't seem too deep—and his arm is clearly broken. His leg looks questionable too, and I know when he walks again there will be an obvious limp.

"It's okay, brother," I say to Noah reassuringly. "I'm gonna go get her. We will all be together very, very soon. You need help first."

I hold his shoulders and feel my tears wash over his wounds.

They close in an instant.

I see her as soon as I am outside, a wounded person hanging on either one of her small, weak shoulders. They weren't made to support that kind of weight, not with her malnutrition. I run to help her and lift one of them on to my own shoulder, realising that the person I help is an injured attacker.

"Riley—" I begin, but she stops me short. For once, I let her.

"He is just as much a person as anybody else here. You don't think he deserves a chance to repent?" It's a rhetorical question, one which I was never meant to argue against. Besides, I don't have an argument anyway, and so I continue to help the man holding on to my shoulder.

He pleads, "I'm sorry, I didn't want to, I never wanted this."

I consider how he was likely under the influence of a dictator much like Thomas, devoid of any mind of his own, any other choice.

"Okay," I say. "Okay."

It takes a while to help all those that we can. In the midst of the smoke, we take Yua's body, along with the fallen who I hadn't been able to reach in time, and we spend an hour burying them close to the Thames. Their graves are marked by a tall tree, one which is starting to spurt new life after the long winter.

I take a moment to thank God no one else was taken.

The rest of the missing take care of the city as we walk to an underground office, the entrance through which is a wooden panel in one of this building's rooms.

Essentially, we are back Underneath.

It's just like our home was, only it's a whole lot bigger and takes forever to unlock.

It's his hidden office, Thomas's, just like my father had. Only, my father was trying to protect those from what he had helped cause. Thomas was trying to continue the damage he didn't know he was creating.

I expect to see a lot of paperwork and nothing else. But instead, there are photos of a young, beautiful woman from years back. Maybe it's his mother. I think it is because there are more photos of a very young boy that resembles Thomas, with the woman and a man. They are all smiling, and the smiles reach their eyes in fullness.

The calm before the storm.

I search for Noah among everybody and there he is, as little as a small scar upon his forehead, looking a lot better than when I had last seen him not long before now.

Liam saved him.

Noah is completely and utterly conscious of my gaze.

He looks up and straightens himself so that he is facing me, weary eye to weary eye.

"No London eye today, I'm afraid." He smirks, dimple upon his left cheek.

"Well, given the circumstances." I sniffle and laugh simultaneously.

Ebony's heavy head leans into my mother's chest. She is battered and bruised, conquered by grief.

"You helped your people," I whisper to her, planting a delicate kiss upon her forehead. "Your mother is still here with us, watching over you with eyes that are no longer glazed." I wait for her response, but she says nothing.

"The war is over now Ebony. No-one else is going to get hurt."

I think I see a smile begin to surface upon her face, but it is gone in moments. She does not seem convinced that the war is over, not completely.

Between silent sobs, she hums *"Be careful what it's like brother, to not have a soul. Looking out of those dead eyes instead of your own."*

Chapter Nineteen

1 Year Later

My eyes open to Noah gently shaking my shoulders. He asks if I am ready. I nod, and he hugs me, his messy hair tickling my neck.

As the four of us step out of the train, I am simultaneously hit with floral air. The wind is stronger out here, though not as strong as it had been during the cold, but brisk and cool. In the distance I can see a mass of flowers, slightly waterlogged from the previous night's rain.

We walk alongside everyone from the camp, and all of the missing. Ebony is sat on Liam's shoulders all the way to grassland area not far from the edge of the ocean, carrying tulips – Yua's favourite flower – in her small palms.

When we reach the grassland, we are greeted by the memorial garden we had been creating for almost half a year in memory of Ebony's mother, Yua.

It is beautiful, depicting her soul through nature.

My father walks over and examines the garden with his arm around my mother. He puts his other hand on my shoulder and says, "I'm proud of you, Ri." Liam looks over and raises an eyebrow. My father laughs and says, "You too, Son. I've never stopped being proud of you both."

Noah walks through the garden gates holding two coffee cups in his hand. I had never tried coffee until a few months ago, and now I seem to be fully educated into every type.

"Latte with pumpkin spice and extra chocolate sprinkles?"

He knows.

"I don't know how you can drink that stuff," Liam pokes his tongue out, mocking his little sister.

"You drink black coffee—which is disgusting by the way—and I am fully accepting of that. Diversity, my brother."

He can't argue against that.

"Doctor Carter—" Noah begins, but my father does the whole informal thing of,

"Please, Noah, we've spoken about this. It's James."

"Sir, my politeness will not waver." He smiles a stupid with his head high, messy hair still messy but somewhat a little less than how it had been when I first met him. It is full of curls but it's been cut slightly so that his eyes stand out more, visible now his fringe is not unruly long and untamed.

"I was wondering if I may borrow your daughter for a moment or two?" Liam smirks at this, and I get the feeling he knows something I do not.

In fact, I think my father does too, because he winks at Noah and says, "Go for it, Son."

The two of us make our way out of the garden and begin walking. It is a long walk, but I don't complain at all. There are less and less buildings and more nature as we walk on, and this is why I am in love with London, because each surrounding area is different to the next.

Finally, we are walking through a place called Hersham Riverside Park, which sits beautifully along the Thames. I am in awe of its peacefulness, yet it's not so calm that there is no sound. I can hear life coming from every tree, every plant.

"Wait, isn't this where—" I don't finish because we have reached what I recognise to be the bush for which I crawled under and found Noah's makeshift ice rink. Only now, there is a wooden door, fairy lights surrounding each tree beside it.

"Noah—"

He opens the door for me, saying, "Ladies first." I am greeted by his grandmother before I can walk in fully, and she tells me to cover my eyes. I do as I am told, heart beating impossibly fast.

It beats even faster when I open them.

Noah

She is warmer than she had been in the summer, her smile full of wonder, delicate under the morning sun. I hand her the baby blue ice skates and she is already flying gracefully along the ice, but she still hasn't noticed the best bit.

"Riley, look," I gesture towards the back of the skating rink. The wooden fencing surrounding the rink then overlooks all nature around us. A dozen deer run free and in awe at their home.

Riley stops what she is doing, her golden eyes wide, her blushed lips in the shape of an 'O' as she gapes and skis over.

I join her and watch too.

She tucks her long, smooth hair behind her ears so that she can get a better view, dark eyelashes catching the light falling of snow.

One deer stops to stare at her. I kind of think I'm imagining it, but I can't be because she sees it too. The deer is looking directly at Riley with eyes full of wonder, and it stays like that for a short moment before running off with the herd.

Riley smiles.

"It kinda reminds me of you," I say.

"Really, why?"

"Just the way it looks at the world. You look at the world like that too." For a moment, her eyes are fixated on mine, her expression unreadable. But all too quickly, she rolls a snowball out of the snow on the fencing and hurls it at me. She laughs and her heart begins to glow inside her chest, lighting up the entire rink. I laugh and my heart feels warm, so I grab her cold hand and she feels it too.

The freckles on her face are the stars constellations. She is the entire cosmos, and I won't ever let people tell her otherwise. She will be used as a thousand lights for everyone, just as we are all destined for good plans if we let them in. Any disease, any illness will make her stronger. She harnesses light so that it flows through everyone.

"Riley," I whisper, all serious now.

"Yes, Noah?"

"There are two types of people in this world. There are the people that seek the wonder and curiosity, and there are the people that try to destroy it because they believe there is only one way to live. You are light in this world; promise you won't ever let the darkness take that away from you."

Riley

I promise.